HOT SEAL, SINGLE MALT

KRIS MICHAELS

WWW.KRISMICHAELSAUTHOR.COM

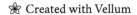 Created with Vellum

COLLECT THE SEALS IN PARADISE SERIES

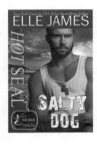

Hot SEAL, Salty Dog
by Elle James
Amazon
Barnes & Noble
Kobo
Apple

Hot SEAL, S*x on the Beach
by Delilah Devlin
Amazon
Barnes & Noble
Kobo
Apple

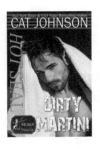

Hot SEAL, Dirty Martini
by Cat Johnson
Amazon
Barnes & Noble
Kobo
Apple

Hot SEAL, Bourbon Neat
by Parker Kincade
Amazon
Barnes & Noble
Kobo
Apple

Hot SEAL, Red Wine
by Becca Jameson
Amazon
Barnes & Noble
Kobo
Apple

Hot SEAL, Cold Beer
by Cynthia D'Alba
Amazon
Barnes & Noble
Kobo
Apple

∽

Hot SEAL, Rusty Nail
by Teresa Eraser
Amazon
Barnes & Noble
Kobo
Apple

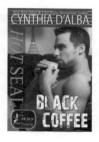

Hot SEAL, Black Coffee
by Cynthia D'Alba
Amazon
Barnes & Noble
Kobo
Apple

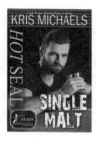

Hot SEAL, Single Malt
by Kris Michaels
Amazon
Barnes & Noble
Kobo
Apple

CHAPTER 1

*G*unner "Iceman" Kincaid stepped out of his Chevy King Cab and ambled up to the keyless entry panel on the garage door of the squat, stucco covered cement brick bungalow he'd purchased from his father about ten years ago. His father had built the three houses tucked away in the secluded cove of Half Moon Bay when Gunner was a kid. The land on the cove was inherited property that Gunner's grandfather had left to his father. The property nestled at the south end of the bay with a panoramic view unimpeded by structures of any kind. The looming cliff line that bordered the small inlet his family owned stood as sentinels against the dynamic and sometimes unforgiving forces of the Pacific Ocean. Dark and looming in the twilight, they never failed to make him feel small. Yet those twin guardians welcomed him back home. He glanced out the garage door to the other houses. Pops still lived in one of them, but the windows were dark. The rental unit sat next door, quiet and dark. He took the time to eye the surrounding natural beauty with an appreciation he'd lacked as a child. The places the Navy had sent him weren't nearly as picturesque.

He keyed his mother's birthdate into the device—she'd died years ago but he still held her memory close—and watched the garage door open, smiling at his 2011 Heritage Softail Classic, now draped by a tarp. He'd missed his fucking Harley almost as much as he missed his old man. Okay, not really, but he loved the bike, too. Gunner chuckled and headed back to pull the truck into the garage. Everything he owned was wrapped up and strapped down in the bed of his Chevy. Not that he'd acquired much in the last twenty years. He hoped to change that now.

Gunner hit the button beside the door that led to the kitchen, and the garage door slid down almost soundlessly. He stopped three steps into the house without turning on a light. The evening view of Half Moon Bay through the kitchen windows snagged his attention and held it. The moon was still visible, sending a swath of pale lemon colored light onto the surface of the water. Further out, he could see the fog bank hovering. The waves were minimal in the cove, but the motion of the water against the sand and pebble beach projected a hypnotic sense of well-being. A sense of calm overtook him as he watched the rhythmic ebb and flow of the waves. The water called to him like a siren's song. *Fuck it, he'd play sailor to the seductress.* He needed to exercise after last night's generous consumption of alcohol and today's eleven-hour and thirty-minute drive from Coronado, California. He tossed his keys in the air, turned on his heel, and headed to his truck. It took him five minutes to change into his wetsuit and find the box that held his goggles and fins. Then he headed out the side door of the garage and padded down to the beach. A fog bank hovered just outside the bay. Gunner refreshed his mind about the cliffs and an old tree, twisted from years of Mother Nature's abuse that he used as reference points before he entered the water. The small rocks that littered the sandy beach reminded him to step carefully. He tucked his fins under his belt, snugged his goggles to his face, and dove in. *Shit!* He'd forgotten how fucking cold the water was. The intense, heart-pounding jolt woke his ass up. He pulled his fins out of his belt and slipped them on his feet. He lowered his goggles and once again confirmed his landmarks. The fog progressively consumed the expanse of ocean water as it rolled onto land. He'd welcomed the seclusion the thick clouds brought. The combination of fog and the currents that lurked outside the bay could be dangerous for an inexperienced or inattentive swimmer. A smile tugged on his lips. Twenty years as a Navy SEAL guaranteed he was neither. He leaned forward, inhaled deeply and submerged, silently pulling himself through the water with strong strokes. He controlled his heart rate to extend his time underwater. Normally, due to his extensive training, he could push closer to three minutes before he had to resurface.

Here, in the embrace of the ocean, peace enveloped him. The small stroke his old man had suffered nine months ago was the crowning factor in his decision to retire. When he hit twenty years and was eligible, Gunner submitted his paperwork, completed his last mission and headed home to Half Moon Bay and the Wayward Walrus, the bar his pops had started in a house he'd reno'd on Main Street. His old man was going to be pissed he'd retired. Pops would think he had sacrificed his career to come home and work in a bar. He didn't feel that way. He was moving on with his life. The decision was solid, and he had no regrets. He needed to package his retirement in the right light and sell it to his old man.

His lungs burned before he resurfaced. Silently, he broke through the water, took a cleansing breath, then two deep breaths, marked his location, and submerged. The cold, black, water enfolded him and left no trace of his presence.

A.J. Ericson's hands shook violently as she pushed the three numbers on her cell. She paced at the water's edge. *This could not be happening!* "Oh my God, oh my God, oh my God! Pick up!"

A woman answered, "Nine-one-one do you have—"

"Yes, I have a fucking emergency! This guy just walked into the bay. It's fucking pitch-black outside. He floated there for a while. I called as I ran down to the beach, but he went under! He never came up! I can't swim well enough to go after him! Oh, my God, I think he drowned!"

"Ma'am I'm going to need you to calm down. Exactly, where are you?"

A.J. sputtered out her address, and the woman repeated it. A.J. acknowledged, "Yes, that's right."

The polite, steady voice continued, "Alright ma'am, I have a deputy en route. What is your name?"

"Amanda Jean Ericson. A.J." She cast her eyes over the surface of the water. Dead people floated right? She clenched her eyes shut and threw that thought away. *No, that... just no.*

"Can you give me a description of the person who went under water?" The woman sounded as if she was asking for the time of day.

How in the hell was this woman so damn calm? "No..." A.J. shook her head and lifted her free hand in the air waving it at the heavens as she spoke, well...okay, maybe yelled, "He was tall and big, I think, but I was so far away! I'd just come home. I wasn't even supposed to be here tonight. I came home for five minutes to grab some paperwork because the inventory was off. I look across the back to the water and

KRIS MICHAELS

see this guy I don't recognize, walking straight into the freezing cold water, and then he just disappears!"

"Alright, ma'am, can you describe his clothing?"

"Seriously, lady, what part of I didn't see him well didn't you hear? I was..." A.J. spun around and looked at the three houses nestled into the coastal landscape at least a thousand yards from the bay. The mist from the bay had started to sneak ashore and transformed everything into a setting from some horror story. She pointed at her house. "I was all the way up there, and the fog is coming in. I can't even see out to the bay anymore." She swiveled back toward the water and shivered. It was *maybe* fifty degrees tonight. The water temperature was always so freaking cold here, nothing like the waters off the coast of Texas where she'd played growing up.

"I understand. Ma'am, we have people en route to help you. Now, do you see anything on the beach? Clothing, a wallet, anything unusual?"

A.J. rolled her eyes at the woman's placid attitude. She drew a deep breath and scrutinized the sandy, pebbled beach. Small round pebbles scattered around the sand made up the beach on this stretch of ocean-front property, and she didn't see any footprints. She couldn't even tell from which direction the man had entered the private property. It was getting so damn dark. A.J. searched the beach she knew so well, but she didn't see anything. The man had left nothing that would indicate he would return. The reality of what had happened hit her. *Someone had walked out into the water with the intention of not returning.* "No. There's nothing here."

A distant high-pitched wail from the direction of the highway drew her attention. She swallowed hard, pushing back the emotion that threatened to swallow her. Her voice trembled as she responded. "I hear them. Tell them to use the access road south of my house. They can pull down to the water."

"Thank you, I'll relay the information. Are you alright? I can stay on the phone with you if you need." This time the woman's voice seemed almost motherly.

A.J. shook her head as she stared into the fog that had obscured the water. "No, I'm okay. I'll wait here."

She disconnected her cell phone and dropped it into her jacket-sweater pocket. What would drive a person to such an act of desperation? It wouldn't matter how rough things got, she'd never commit suicide. She'd fought hard *not* to die. The siren of the responding police car cut off as it approached the houses. She watched the blue lights bounce off the low hanging mist and the arc of the headlights when they cut through the darkness. She knew the instant the car started its drive down the faint access road Silas used to get the massive lawnmower to the lower forty, as he called the expanse of land between the houses and the water.

She shielded her eyes against the glare of the headlights as the vehicle pulled to a stop, spotlighting her. She heard the door open rather than saw it, thanks to the temporary blindness from the headlights.

"A.J., what's going on?" *That* voice she recognized immediately.

She blinked repeatedly trying to clear the spots from her vision. Before she could see him, she vomited the information she'd already told the 911 operator. "Delmont, there was a guy. I saw him from the street as I getting in my car to leave. He walked straight into the water. I could see him floating for a moment. Shit, it scared me, you know? We had those two tourists die from the undertow outside the bay a while back, and I freaked, so I came running down here. I yelled at him. Either he didn't hear me or ignored me. He went under the water, right there." She pointed to a spot about ten yards away from shore. "He never came up. I waited and waited. God, maybe three or four minutes before I called 911. Did I wait too long?"

"No, you did fine, A.J." His voice carried a professional edge to it, and for once it didn't get her back up. She welcomed it. Delmont Johnson was one of the first people she met when she arrived in Half Moon Bay. A meeting neither cared to talk about. He glanced down the beach. "Did you see who it was?"

"No, I couldn't, it was too far away. He was tall and big." She lifted her shoulders and held out her arms indicating a big chest and arms.

She watched as he lit the searchlight attached to the driver's side door. The powerful light barely cut through the fog over the water. The blue flashing lights of his light bar bounced against the mist following the swirls of cotton candy thick clouds that pulsed onto land from the ocean.

"Stay here, I'm going to take a look." He slid into the vehicle and moved his car forward slowly, sending the searchlight in a pattern along the beach. She watched as he cast the illumination as far out into the water as the beam would penetrate. A.J. shivered. The moisture of the fog coupled with the cool climate of the coastline dampened her clothes, making them useless against the elements. The trembling was also from the emotional shock of witnessing what might prove to be a suicide.

Delmont turned the car and slowly worked his way back to her, searching as far as he could see. He parked the vehicle, leaving the spotlight aimed at the ocean. A.J. could hear him talking on the radio, just the low rumble of his voice and the distorted reply of the same woman she'd spoken to earlier. He opened the car door and headed her way. They were both illuminated by his headlights and highlighted by the bouncing blue lights. He took off his cowboy hat and rubbed the back of his neck as he did a three-sixty of the area. "The fog is too thick to launch Search and Rescue. I had dispatch call the Coast Guard and the County team. Everything is grounded."

She understood keeping the first responders safe, but... "Then what do we do?" Her voice cracked. *Damn it, someone was out there.*

Delmont put a hand on her shoulder and squeezed, offering support. "I can't see more than three or four yards into the water. All we can do is pray the guy decided he wanted to live and came ashore somewhere else. Other than that, we wait until we can see, and then we launch a recovery operation."

"Recovery and not rescue?" AJ swallowed hard.

"What the fuck is going on?"

AJ nearly fell on her ass as she spun back toward the water. A colossal, super-sized man wearing a black wetsuit marched out of the water. He held fins in his left hand, his right-hand snatched goggles off his forehead.

"Del? Man look at you! A deputy sheriff, who the hell would have thought that could happen?"

"Iceman? Holy fuck dude, do you know how much you scared us?"

AJ spun toward Delmont and then back toward the asshole that had taken ten fucking years off her life and left her a quivering wreck.

CHAPTER 2

"*W*hat are you talking about?" For the first time, Gunner glanced at the woman standing with Delmont. She was a tiny thing. Five foot nothing if she was an inch. When she swung her head from Delmont to him, her ponytail whipped around and slapped her in the face. She was a cute thing...

"You stupid, meat-headed asshole! I called 911 because of you. What the hell were you doing? Don't you know those waters are dangerous? I thought you were committing suicide! Two people drowned here last week. What were you trying to prove? What right do you have to even be here? Shit... I *am not* crying over some stupid asshole." The woman swiped at her cheeks. "I can't believe this!"

Gunner lifted his hand and opened his mouth to respond, but the little firecracker kept going, rather like a Smurfy version of a chainsaw. He snapped his mouth shut when she held up a finger at him and shook it.

"No, you don't have any right! None! You're trespassing! Of all the stupid, idiotic things to do! Haven't you heard about safety? Going swimming at night, in the fog, without anyone on shore, and on private property! Can you spell riptide? No? Well, let me help you. S.T.U.P.I.D! That is what this stunt was! Beyond dumb. Absolutely insane." She spun and started marching up the expanse of land toward the street where Gunner saw a red Miata parked. She yelled over her shoulder, "Delmont, arrest this man for...hell, I don't care what you arrest him for, but do it! If you have anything for me to sign you know where to find me!"

Gunner channeled some of that inner Zen that got him his Iceman nickname back in high school. Others got stressed, but not much fazed him. He'd learned not to give life to make that much power over him. His eyes followed the cute ass packed into those tight jeans all the way up the hill and monitored her progression between the two houses. The fog ruined his view at that point. He could still hear her ranting and raving, though. No amount of fog would deafen that angry tirade. He turned toward Delmont. "What's up?" It seemed like a place to start. There were so many more questions, like who was the pissed-off pipsqueak? Why was Delmont here; and why would he get arrested for being on his own property?

"Well, I believe we had a misunderstanding. Did you tell anyone you were visiting?" The radio in the squad car cackled, and Delmont held up his hand before Gunner could answer.

Well, that shit was happening all too frequently. First *Thumbelina* and then Delmont, in a matter of three minutes. Gunner glanced around the private beach as Del went back to his car. The blue lights stopped suddenly putting the area into a darker hue.

Del spoke into his mic, "Dispatch you can show me clear out here. No incident, property owner taking a swim. You'll need to call the Coast Guard and the County Search and Rescue team and let them know there isn't anything for them to do when the fog burns off."

"Roger that. The sheriff came in when we made the notification. I'm sure he'll want an out-brief, Del."

"Affirm. I'll be heading towards the station in a couple minutes." Del strode back toward Gunner.

Gunner motioned towards the water. "She thought I'd drowned out there?" He laughed at that. Probably inappropriate, but damn, that shit was funny. "Del, I swear if BUD/S training and Hell Week didn't manage that task, there is no way in hell a casual swim in calm waters would take me out.

"Big, badass SEAL." Del chuckled too before he cleared his throat and continued, "Pretty sure she didn't know about your training. Dude, when did you get back in town?"

Gunner dropped his fins and dug his bare feet

deeper into the wet sand, keeping them warm while he and Del spoke. "I pulled in about five minutes before I dove in the water. I'd been driving all fucking day. Needed to stretch and exercise. How in the hell did a passerby see me?"

"Passerby?" Del blinked at him like he was insane.

"Yeah, wait, does she live around here?"

There had been some talk about a couple houses going up to the south of Pop's land. He did know the county had extended the road that passed these houses to the south about three years ago. Last time he was home, he'd jogged it, then hooked west and looped back to the east on the backroads. The circuit he cut was five miles. He jogged it once and then ran it, full out. A decent run, although not very taxing.

"Does she live around here?" Del parroted.

"Dude, having problems hearing?" Gunner unzipped the wetsuit to his waist.

Delmont chuckled and then laughed before he answered. "No, *dude*, I'm not having any problems hearing you. Yes, she lives around here, and I'm assuming since you didn't answer me that your old man does not know you're home."

"I didn't answer because you held up that stop sign sized mitt of yours and left to take care of business." Gunner motioned toward Delmont's hands when he reminded the man of his silent command for silence. "No, I didn't tell Dad. He didn't need to worry about my coming back."

"Hey, these hands got me a free ride to college. So, you're back to stay?"

"Best damn wide receiver I had the privilege of throwing a ball to." Gunner acknowledged. "Yeah, I put in my papers. I'm on terminal leave. In eighty-nine days, I will be a retired Navy SEAL."

"Where is your old man?" Delmont looked up at the old family house. "I assume since he's not here he's either at the pub or...?"

"He went into San Francisco. He has a routine test tomorrow morning. Told me he was going to go into the city today, so he didn't have to face rush hour traffic." Gunner rolled his shoulders. "Hey, listen, if you aren't going to arrest me for being on my own property, I'm going to head up, unpack what I brought with me and get some shut-eye. It was a long night last night."

"Retirement party?"

"Nah, kinda a thing for a friend of mine. Probably the last time I'll see those guys, so it lasted a while."

"I get that. And to answer your question, no I'm not arresting you. Although I should to avoid her wrath." Delmont motioned toward the street.

"She's new in town?" Gunner grew up in Half Moon Bay. Twelve thousand residents on a good day. Sure, people come and go, but he'd have remembered if he'd seen that tea-cup sized tornado. People like her, he'd definitely notice, and not just because of her force of nature personality. That woman would turn his head if she never said a word. She was point-blank beautiful.

"New-ish. I guess she showed up about a year ago." Delmont shrugged. "Maybe a bit less, I can't remember. She's a live wire and won't take shit off of anyone."

"My kind of woman." Gunner smiled and cuffed Delmont on the back. "Let's meet up and have a drink sometime."

"At the Walrus?" Delmont lowered his big frame into the patrol car and looked up at Gunner.

"Yeah, that would be best since I came home to take over the operation. Dad had to hire some temporary help to run the bar after his stroke. I figured we can let the guy go once I get my bearings."

Delmont blinked up at him and laughed again. "Iceman, you really need to talk to Pops more. I'll be seeing you around, and I'll take you up on that drink, but I'm buying. What's your drink nowadays? Sure as hell hope it ain't still Boone's Farm apple wine."

Gunner groaned at the memory of *that* epic hang-over. Sixteen-years-old, three friends and six bottles of wine they got a college kid to buy for them, resulted in one of the worst headaches he'd ever had, and that said one hell of a lot. "I'm a single malt guy now."

Delmont snorted. "Figures, you pull out the expensive tastes *after* I say I'm buying." He shut the door and dropped his elbow out the open window. " I don't want to come back out here tonight for a trespassing call, so in case your dad didn't tell you, he has a renter. My number's in the book, or you can reach me through dispatch. It's good to have you home, Iceman."

Gunner waved as Delmont backed up, and he headed to his house. He entered through the side garage door he'd exited from and flipped on the light. Time to dry off and then get to work unpacking.

CHAPTER 3

A.J. sat back on her heels. The count was wrong. Either the inventory had been doctored, or the vendors were shorting them. She sighed and looked at the clipboard again. She'd gone over everything last night, twice, and again this morning. Ten bottles of top-shelf, ten bottles of house liquor and five cases of beer. She tapped the clipboard with her pen. How long had the inventory been off? She glanced down at the signature of the employee that had conducted this month's count. She flipped the top page of the inventory to the receiving documentation. A different employee signed acceptance for the shipments of alcohol and beer. So, two employees who counted the offload by the vendors stated there was more inventory than the one who counted the stock. Someone was stealing.

She glanced up at the camera that sat quietly in the corner of the room. She knew the system was there recording the bar and storeroom's activity. Silas had it installed when there was a rash of burglaries about four years ago. The footage was kept in the cloud for a year and then vanished. The back door opened, and A.J. lifted off the floor, rising out of a surround of the open boxes of alcohol.

"Anyone home?" Silas's bellow put a smile on her face in an instant.

"Just us gremlins!" She made her way to the coffee pot because that is where Silas would be.

He turned and lifted the pot in her direction asking silently if she wanted a cup. He looked good. Dressed in black slacks and a button-down, she could see how much weight he'd lost recently. His hazel eyes twinkled at her. He flopped his grey hair out of his eyes and waited for a response.

"God, yes. Please." She slid into the small banquet seat at the rear of the bar they'd claimed during the hours the pub was closed. "How did the appointments go?"

"Fine, or that is what the doctors are telling me. The meds are doing what they are supposed to do."

A.J. had worked for Silas for just over seven months. Just before she came aboard, he'd suffered a minor stroke—if any stroke could be called minor. The event had forced him to advertise for a bar manager. Due to a fatally toxic relationship, A.J. needed to relocate. It was karma, or fate, or hell, just good damn luck. She had liked Silas immediately, and they meshed well. So well that two months ago,

A.J. had made an offer to buy twenty percent of the bar. Silas agreed, and the papers were signed last month. A.J. had found a permanent home in Half Moon Bay.

"So, they didn't change anything?" Silas underplayed his medical condition. If she had to pull the information out of him, she was tenacious enough to do it. Just because she was small didn't mean she wasn't fierce.

Silas slid her mug across the table as he sat down with his. "They gave me a different pill. Supposed to control some of the issues better than the one I was on before. They lowered the dose on the blood thinners, too. Scheduled me for another appointment in a month to re-evaluate. The doc said overall, he was happy with my labs but wanted to get them perfect, and that was why he was switching the meds. Says some people respond better to different types." He shrugged. "He also said the exercise that we're doing is improving my overall health. He was impressed with the weight loss. Five more pounds this month. Said he'd like to see me continue it, lose another twenty to twenty-five pounds."

Happiness draped her shoulders and snuggled around her like a fluffy blanket. "That's amazing! I love going for our walks before work. I hope you're not thinking about stopping."

"Wouldn't dream of it. I'm hooked. I can see my shoes without bending over. That hasn't happened in way too many years. Besides, I like the attention I'm getting from the ladies now." He winked at her and his booming laughter echoed in the empty pub. Silas had himself a small harem of older, single ladies who appeared regularly at the pub. A.J. smiled at him and shook her head. He was an adorable teddy bear and an amazing business partner and friend. "So how was business last night?"

"Business was on par. Receipts are about a hundred over normal, so I'm not going to complain, especially for a Monday night." A.J. pulled her bottom lip into her mouth and narrowed her eyes at her business partner. "Couple things I need to talk to you about, though."

Silas sat his coffee cup down and leaned back in the seat. "Why do I not like that tone?"

"Probably because you're a smart man." A.J. took another sip of her coffee.

Silas lifted an eyebrow. "Quit buttering me up and hit me with it."

"First, I had to pop home last night to grab last month's inventory from the files. I'll tell you why in a moment, but when I was getting back into my car I saw a man walk into the bay."

"Out at our place?" Silas interjected his question.

"Yeah. Either he was too far away to hear me when I called out to him, or he ignored me." A.J. realized the man was even more of a douchebag than she'd pegged him because he probably did ignore her. Damn, she hoped Del had arrested him. Hoped he had to post bail, too. Silas lifted his coffee to his lips breaking her from her thoughts. She shook her head. "Anyway, he disappeared under the water. I freaked when he didn't resurface. I called the cops. Del showed up. We searched, but the fog rolled in so thick that we couldn't see anything."

Silas stared at her in disbelief. "Dammit. Do they have search and rescue out there now?"

A.J. snorted. "No. Just when Del was telling me all the teams were grounded because of the fog, the guy walks out of the water, all casual, like he had no idea why there was a police car on the beach. The idiot. God! The man trespasses on private property and has the audacity to look like he doesn't have a care in the world."

She saw Silas's shoulders move as he suppressed his laughter, "Bet that set you off."

A.J. scrunched up her nose at him. "He deserved it. I thought he was attempting suicide or had drowned." She snorted. "I told Del to arrest him...I don't know what kind of charges he could put on the guy, but I know he trespassed at least."

Silas lifted his coffee cup and smiled as he brought the cup to his lips. "I think trespass without extenuating circumstances is just a citation."

"Really? Well, hell, that's not right." She took another sip of her coffee. "Anyway, that asshole aside, I think we have a problem."

"Something to do with last month's inventory?" Silas sat his coffee cup down and clasped his hands in front of him.

"Yeah, like I said last night was par for a Monday night, so I had time on my hands. One of the things that Henshaw used to do when I worked for him as manager was to go through some of the responsibilities he'd given his employees. He told me more than once if the boss didn't keep involved in the process the process could take over the boss. So, I did an OSHA inspection. There was a fire extinguisher that needed recharging and hadn't been signed off on, which isn't huge, but..."

"It would have earned us a write-up." Silas nodded.

A.J. sighed, "Yeah, so then I pulled the inventory sheet. Figured it would fill a half hour or so."

"I take it by the expression on your face that it filled far more than a half hour." He tipped his head waiting for her to explain.

"Yes. I had to go to my house to get the files." Silas had allowed her to take the documentation home. She'd wanted to make sure her buying into the pub was a sound business decision, and she'd gone over the files for the last three years. Every page and every document was scoured for information before she pulled a draw on her inheritance.

She nodded her head toward the stack of boxes in the corner. "Brought them back today. Anyway, after all the crap with the dude at the beach, I returned and did a count. The inventory we brought in minus the use does not equal what we are supposed to have on hand."

Silas leaned forward. "Just how much is missing?"

"According to my count?" He nodded, his eyes expressing the concern she shared. "Ten bottles of top shelf, ten of house and five cases of beer."

"So, a sizeable amount." Silas leaned back and drew a deep breath.

"Yep, but I want you to go through the documentation and do a count. I'd like to make sure my conclusions are correct."

"We can pull up the security feed." He scrubbed his hand over his cheek and chin. "I don't even remember my password for the system. Installed it and never used it."

"I'm sure we can get it from the company." A.J. nodded to the boxes again. "While you're counting and contacting the company, I'll put the files away and mop again. Whatever Amy used on the floor last night left a haze on the tile." She glanced down at the floor and frowned at the mess.

"Well, I guess we both have work to do before we open in ..." Silas glanced at his watch, "... an hour and a half."

"August will be here in an hour. I'd like to have it all done by the time he shows up for his shift so we don't have a rumored issue involved. If whoever is stealing finds out we are aware, they could bolt or cover their tracks. To that end, I stayed after closing last night to do the count and then came in early today to do it again." A.J. grabbed one of the file boxes as Silas grabbed the other.

Silas sighed, "Then we need to get after it. Come on co-owner, we need to roll up sleeves and get after it."

Gunner twisted the throttle letting the motorcycle fly. He'd unpacked last night, showered and slept like the dead. As the sun was rising this morning, he went for a run along the same course he'd taken the last time he was home. There were houses built along the road. His imagination ran free as he ran, wondering in which house the fiery little woman lived. He passed a house with children's toys outside and grimaced, admitting that she could be married. Someone that vibrant and beautiful was bound to be attached. Damn, he wished he'd been able to see her better last night. The headlights shaded her features, but he could tell her hair was auburn or a dark chestnut brown. Her eyes were either blue or light green and her body...fuck, her body was banging. Tight ass, small waist and he'd lie if he said he didn't notice the way her chest heaved when she was yelling at him, even under the shapeless sweater thing she wore.

He thought about her now as he slowed and maneuvered his bike through some light traffic. He needed to come back into town later this afternoon and stock up on food, but the diner on the edge of town had sufficed for breakfast...and probably lunch...the diner had never shorted people on food, but the omelet, bacon, hash browns and side order of pancakes almost beat him. Almost.

He smiled as he turned onto Main Street. The town hadn't changed much. A few new buildings and paint color changes on others. As he neared the Walrus, he smiled. He hadn't seen his old man in almost two years. He passed the pub and noticed the new white paint and widened porch that now had small bistro tables situated outside. The patio was lined with lush green plants and strings of old Edison bulbs hung over head. It looked amazing. Nosing the bike into a parking slot about a block down from the pub, he pulled off his helmet and ran a hand through his hair and beard. He'd shaved when the team had gotten back about two weeks ago before he out-processed, but he was letting it grow back. He'd grown accustomed to it during deployments when shaving was the absolute last thing any of them had to worry about. Now, it was full and, as of this morning, trimmed to be presentable. He glanced at the pub again. The open sign was still dark. Gunner swung off, attached the helmet to the bike and locked it down. Not that he didn't trust people, but the helmet had a custom paint job. He wasn't going to tempt fate.

Gunner stretched and headed to the back door of the pub. Man, he couldn't wait to see the expression on his old man's face. A smile broke as he strode to the steps. He avoided a mop that had been casually propped at the bottom step. It was wet and smelled of cleaner. Shit. His dad damn well better not be doing custodial work. Gunner's good mood vanished as he heard an eerily familiar voice, "Did you get the same numbers?"

Gunner shook his head. No, it couldn't be. He put his foot on the bottom stair as the door opened. "What? Wait just a minute while I get rid of this."

He paused. No, *that was* the same voice as last night. He heard the door open and moved to the left before he lifted onto the second step, not wanting to be concealed when she exited. God knew he didn't want to scare her again.

He looked up just as a wall of grey water launched from the door. Instinctively he closed his eyes and braced. The tepid water swamped him as he turned his head. He felt the initial slap of water followed by the instantaneous absorption of the liquid into the fabric of his clothes. Gunner hung his head and opened his eyes. Small rivulets of water turned into huge drops as he released his breath.

"Oh, my God! I'm so sorry! I didn't know you were back here. Wait, why are you back here?"

Gunner used his hand as a squeegee to push his hair back and protect his eyes from the antiseptic smell of the water. As he lifted his head, he heard a gasp.

"You! What are you doing here? If you're trying to get me not to press charges, you are barking up the wrong tree, mister. I have half a mind to call Deputy

Johnson. I don't know much about the law but following me is harassment...or stalking!"

"Is everything alright?" His dad's voice echoed down the hall that led to the offices, stockroom, and employee break room.

Gunner swiped the water away from his face and whipped his wrist sending it to the wall of the building with a splat. He opened his mouth to respond to his father, but Minnie-Mouth beat him to the punch.

She shouted back, "No, that guy I told you about from last night is here."

Gunner lifted up to the next step. "If you would stop talking long enough for me to—"

"Stop. You better get back before I kick your ass, mister." The little piece of fluff in front of him dropped into a pretty damn respectable fighting stance.

He had her by *at least* a hundred pounds, fourteen or fifteen inches and a lifetime of experience in hand-to-hand combat. He smiled and then started to laugh. The woman was a pistol. He laughed harder and moved up to the third step. His old man was in the bar, and he'd be able to settle the hissing kitten down. Obviously, they knew each other.

"Are you laughing at me? Did Marcus send you?"

In hindsight, Gunner should have recognized the growl in her voice, but damn, the woman was on drugs if she thought... Pain the likes of which he'd avoided his entire life shot through him. Searing lightning bolts flashing behind his eyelids. He dropped his hands to his junk and gasped for air that had been forcibly expelled from his lungs. *Ohmygodshedidnotjustkickmeinthefuckingnuts!*

"I warned you, asshole! Silas! Call the cops!"

Gunner lifted his head and glared at the woman. Or tried to, fuck he couldn't breathe. Those thoughts about her being beautiful, yeah, they flew out the window. He narrowed his eyes at her and let his displeasure out in a low, dangerous rumble. It was instinct. He saw the instant the pint-sized Bruce Lee recognized her mistake. Her eyes widened the same second she went pale. Gunner pierced her with a glare and moved to stand up. Slowly.

"Look, you asked for it." She held out her hand and backed away from him into the pub. "Silas! Silas!"

Gunner cringed as he lifted his leg and stepped onto the landing, but he did it anyway. "My father raised me to treat a lady right, but you...you aren't a lady, you are a fucking wrecking ball." His voice came out three octaves higher than his normal baritone. He didn't care.

"Gunner?" His old man came out of the office with a phone stuck to his ear and a baseball bat in the other hand.

The woman did that ponytail whip around thing again as she snapped her head towards his old man. "Wait. What? Gunner as in your son who is in the Navy? That Gunner?"

Silas nodded and threw down the bat and hung

up the phone. "What the hell happened? Why are you all wet?"

"I'm more concerned about the size-three boot that ruptured my nuts." Gunner was still bent like a question mark, but he managed to glare at the woman. How in the world could he have imagined she was someone he'd like to get to know better?

"What?" Silas moved around the pocket-sized calamity and grabbed his elbow. "You kicked him in the...A.J what possessed you?"

"He *laughed* at my warning, and he kept coming up the stairs. I thought he was...what was I supposed to do? I didn't know he was your son!" Gunner winced as her voice peaked high enough to call every dog in a four-block radius.

His old man grabbed ahold of him and gave him a hug. The embrace was awkward in his current bent position. "Damn son, let a person know you're coming next time."

"No shit," Gunner groaned. He returned the hug even though he was drenching his father in the process.

His dad gave him a couple solid thuds on the back, cleared his throat and pulled away before he threw a command over his shoulder. "A.J. go get a bag of ice." Gunner watched her spin and sprint down the hallway.

"Who the fuck is that?" Gunner pointed down the now empty hallway.

"That is Amanda Jean Ericson, also known as A.J. Come on, let's get you inside."

Gunner held up a finger and bent over placing both hands on his knees.

"Damn, she got you good, didn't she?"

"Seriously, Pops? I'm not appreciating the humor. Men do not laugh at other men who've been racked. That is an unwritten and sacred code."

He looked up and cast a glance down the long tiled hallway when he heard something slam in the bar. "Is she one of your bartenders?" He straightened slowly and walked through the door his father held open.

Silas shut the door behind him and chuckled, "Well she does tend bar occasionally, but she's—"

The woman in question sprinted back down the hall. She slammed to a stop and slipped on water he'd either dripped on the floor or had sloshed out of her bucket. Her right foot skimmed across the tile and, with a thwack of leather against leather, connected with his ankle. Not being steady on his feet after the recent nut crushing incident, he braced against the wall to catch his balance. The ice she carried in a towel smacked him in the chest, pelting him, while dime-sized pieces of frozen water slid down the open collar of his wet shirt and collected around his waist. *Fucking perfect.* The woman was a walking, talking, disaster. One who in any conceivable version of the future, he would avoid like the plague.

"Oh, my God! I'm so sorry!" She reached toward

him. Now that he understood the underhanded methods of his adversary, his well-honed reflexes for self-preservation kicked in, and he jerked away from her touch. Enough of this shit. There was no Zen to be found at this moment, and his renowned calm demeanor disintegrated. He stood up to his full height pulled his shirt out of his jeans, and ripped the buttons open to dislodge the ice around his waist. She covered her mouth and whispered, "I...how can I apologize?"

Gunner stood there, balls aching, drenched, and half dressed. He glared at the walking disaster and shook his head before he spoke. "Lady, stay as far away from me as humanly possible, and I'll call it even."

She nodded, spun on her heel and walked with her back ramrod straight back down the hallway.

His dad cupped him on the shoulder nodded to his office. "Come on, I keep pub t-shirts in my office. We had a guy work for us that wore an XXL, might be tight on those guns you have, but at least it will be dry."

Gunner followed his father into his office and gingerly eased into the first chair he found. "Seriously, *who* is that woman?" He pulled off his shirt and dropped it on the floor with a ripe, juicy splat. The front of his jeans were soaked, but the back was dry and shouldn't hurt the leather chair he'd settled in.

"Do you want the long answer or the short one?"

Gunner's eyes drew up at the serious tone of his

father's response. His gut clenched, and he swallowed hard. "Fuck, Dad, please tell me you're not involved with her?"

There was a chuff of laughter as his dad pulled open an old metal file cabinet and rummaged through the contents. "Well, I guess that depends on your definition of involved." His old man pulled a t-shirt out of the drawer, tossed it to him and pointed to the small bathroom attached to his office. "Towels are freshly laundered in there. Go clean up. I'll pop down to the store and get you a pair of jeans. What size are you wearing nowadays?"

Gunner shook his head and carefully stood up from where he'd been sitting. "Excuse me just a minute, Dad. Is there more than one definition of involved? Honestly, I don't think I can deal with her as a stepmother."

His dad smiled that shit eating grin he got when he won an argument or knew something someone else didn't. The same one Gunner had been accused of using on too many occasions to count. "There are plenty of definitions of involved, but I'm not in a physical relationship with her if that's what you're asking."

The things that had tightened inside Gunner released with those words. Good, at least his dad was safe from the natural disaster masquerading as a female. "It was, and thank God you're not involved with her. She's deadly."

His dad headed to the office door "She's really not. Just intense. Now, what size?"

"Thirty-four waist. Thirty-six-inch inseam, but I can make a thirty-four inseam work if that's all they have." Hell, wear them low on his hips and tuck them in his boots so they didn't look like he'd survived a flood if need be. A smile almost broke through his current foul mood at the thought. He *had* survived a flood. Tropical Storm A.J. had doused him good.

His dad stopped at the door and turned around, a brilliant smile on his face. "I'm sorry about the welcoming committee, but I'm damn glad you're home, son. How long do I have you for?"

Gunner smiled and opened his arms wide. He knew he looked a mess, but he didn't care. "I'm home for good, Pops. I put in my papers. You're stuck with me."

His father's smile faltered. "Seriously? Why?"

Gunner dropped his arms. He looked his dad dead in the eye. "Why? Because it was time, Dad. I've got my twenty in. I've survived some shit I probably shouldn't have, and I want to spend time with you."

His dad just stood there. Gunner's gut sank. "That's okay, isn't it?"

His dad nodded and cleared his throat. "As long as you can promise me it wasn't because of my health. I'm doing a damn good job at managing that."

He could see the pride in his dad's stance. He'd never take that away from his old man, but he couldn't do less than tell the truth. "I'm not going to lie. Your stroke was one of the reasons I considered, but it was only one. Like I said, it was time. I thought it through and weighed my options. I'm honest when I say I would have dropped my paperwork either way. I guess your health made me feel a little, I don't know, needed, maybe, knowing I could maybe help you out around here."

His dad stared at him, no doubt looking for anything that would lead him to believe Gunner was here out of obligation rather than want. He wouldn't find it. He'd wanted to come home. He'd wanted to spend time with his old man. Granted he would always miss his team and the family they'd become, but it was time for him to walk away.

Finally, his father's hand moved away from the door and Gunner found himself wrapped in another embrace. "I'm so glad you're home, kiddo."

Gunner laughed. "I'm forty-years-old. I stopped being a kid eons ago."

His dad stepped back and ruffled Gunner's hair. "You'll always be my kid. Now, go shower, you smell like mop water."

"Yeah? I think there might be a reason for that." Gunner tossed the comment over his shoulder. His extra-thick, double-cushioned, cotton, athletic socks, now water-sodden, squelched and flapped on the tile with every step he took—all the way to the bathroom. No false advertising here. They were super absorbent.

CHAPTER 4

a.J. waited until Silas left to buy some dry
clothes for his son before she moved to the
back hall to clean up the mop water and melting ice.
She shook her head in disbelief. No wonder the man
had looked at her like she was insane last night. Oh,
God, she'd asked Delmont to arrest him. Why hadn't
Delmont said something? Seriously, none of this
would have happened if he'd just piped up and said
something. A.J. sat back on her heels and looked for
any errant melting pieces of ice. "No, you still would
have soaked him in mop water." She spoke out loud
to herself. She'd own that, but if she knew he wasn't a
psycho, she wouldn't have kicked him in his privates.

She crumpled onto her ass and wrapped her arms
around her legs sitting amongst the litter of wet
paper towels that surrounded her. Leave it to her to
compound the errors. Her father had always said
when she did something, she did it big. When she'd

slipped and poured ice all over him? That was an accident. Pure and simple. Not her fault. *Right?*

God, talk about a klutz. She ran through the events up to the point where he'd ripped off his shirt like the Amazing Hulk. Holy hotness he had a gorgeous body. That man was some kinda good-looking. Thick dark brown hair. Beard the same color and framing sinfully sexy lips. Well, they were sexy until he scowled and demanded she stay as far away from him as humanly possible. Lord, the anger that had flashed in his dark brown eyes. Not that she blamed him. He had every right to be mad and tell her to get lost. Hell, *she* didn't want to be around *herself* at the moment.

Her mind kept flashing back to when he'd shredded his shirt and exposed his chest and abdominals. The man was ripped, like movie-star ripped. God, that bronzed expanse of skin would leave any girl's panties wet, especially his Adonis belt...those veed muscles that went lower...merciful heavens...*to the place you kicked him*. She put her hands to her face and groaned.

This was Gunner. The Gunner. Silas's only son. The man she heard wonderful stories about. The pictures she'd seen of him fresh out of basic with a shaved head and looking so terribly young in his Navy whites, held little to no resemblance to the massive man she'd seen last night and today. He looked nothing like Silas. Gunner was dark where Silas was fair. Gunner was taller and more muscled than his father, and his facial features did not bear any resemblance to Silas. None. *How was she supposed to know?* Not that it mattered now. Her pattern of behavior was all too familiar. She'd not only burned the bridge, but as her daddy would say, she'd blown up the road leading to the damn thing. Well, she was nothing if not consistent. She'd preemptively elimi-nated any possibility of a congenial relationship with the man. Hell, he'd asked her to stay away from him. Not sure how she was going to do that when she owned part of the Walrus. Amanda picked up the paper towels and tossed them. She passed the break-room and stopped. The fresh pot of coffee she'd brewed beckoned to her with a wonderful aroma. She tossed her cold coffee into the sink and turned on the faucet to rinse out the cup before glancing up to the clock on the wall. August would be here in ten minutes or so, and then she and Silas could review the security tapes for the last three months. They should have downloaded by now.

But...Silas would want to spend some time with his son on his first full day back. She'd go through the tapes by herself. It wasn't as if Silas *needed* to review them with her. She'd just pop into his office and email the files to her computer. Problem solved, and Silas and Gunner could spend the day, or heck even a couple days, together to catch up.

With that plan firmly in hand, she poured another cup of coffee and headed to Silas's office. She tapped gently on the door and waited. Nothing. She knocked a little louder. Still no response. A.J. opened the door a crack. "Hello?" When no one responded she popped her head in the door and looked around the office. There was no one. She stepped in and listened. There was no sound coming from the bathroom. Maybe Gunner had left? That didn't make any sense. Maybe he went with Silas? *Whatever.* She was going to be firmly planted in her office and away from Silas's son by the time they got back. She went to the desk, woke up Silas's computer and emailed the files to herself.

As she stood up, the door to the bathroom opened. "Oh, I...ah..." Somehow, she lost the ability to talk or think. Gunner filled the bathroom doorway— wearing nothing but a wholly inadequate white towel. Holy Moly! The man was gorgeous, and if the bulge in that towel was any indication, well-endowed to boot.

And that is enough of that! "Sorry, I just needed some files. I knocked. I swear I did. Yeah...ah...just leaving now." She moved two steps toward the door and stopped with a jerk. With an apologetic mutter of, "Coffee," she reached back and grabbed at her coffee cup but managed to contact only the lip of the cup, not the handle. She saw it happening in slow motion. The cup teetered, rocked on the edge of the desk. *No, no, no, no!* She scrambled to catch it before it tipped. Her hand swatted the porcelain, batting it toward Gunner. If coffee cups could fly, this cup was a damn bald eagle soaring in flight. It drifted up, tumbling as it went. A spray of coffee filled the air, all heading straight toward the bathroom door. A.J. jumped forward in some kind of superhero inspired dream of catching the damn thing before it shattered into a million pieces. She hit the floor, knocking the wind out of herself, at the same time the mug detonated and scattered a billion shards of razor-sharp remains over the office floor. A.J. lifted her head and surveyed the remnants of Coffee-agedon. Her eyes landed on the bare, coffee-soaked feet not more than six inches from her nose. Her gaze traveled to his ankles and noticed the stream of coffee that trickled down the light covering of hair on his shin. Her eyes migrated up. Why, she'd never know, because good God have mercy, everything under the towel was on full display. Her initial assessment had been accurate. *Wow.*

"I'd move to protect your modesty, but I'd rather not be picking glass out of my feet for the next week." His frigid voice snapped her out of her trance.

Her gaze plummeted to the ground and stayed there. She could feel her face flame. A.J. pushed up and her eyes bounced all over the room, anywhere but at him. "I'll...I'll go get the broom." She hustled toward the office door, not looking back. She scooted out and slammed the door shut. A.J. clenched her eyes closed and leaned against the door. *I'm going to hell. I'm the worst person. I was checking out his package.* The picture of that long, thick, uncircumcised cock, hanging over his unbruised balls—she'd looked pretty closely, they hadn't appeared bruised—was seared into her corneas.

Silas opened the back door and paused when he saw her leaning against his office door. He raised his eyebrows in question.

A.J. shook her head. "Don't ask. Please, let me go to my office and shut my door. I'll be there all night watching the security video. Tell your son I promise I won't come out. Just, please take him out for dinner or something, I got this." She took two steps and stopped. "Oh, you'll need to take a broom and dustpan with you when you go into your office." She didn't wait for a response, just hightailed it to her office like rabid dogs were on her heels.

~

Gunner pushed away his plate and leaned back in the dark red leather booth at the local steakhouse. It was a local haunt and off of the beaten path. Most of the tourists that flocked to the area didn't know about it. Several times during dinner people had interrupted them, stopping to say hello, welcome him home or just spend a few minutes visiting.

"So, no more pussyfooting around the subject. Tell me about Hurricane A.J." Gunner finished the last of his water.

His father nodded. "Fair enough. This will probably require alcohol." He lifted a finger and ordered them both a double shot of single malt. "After the stroke, the Walrus was too much for me. I didn't want to tell you that, knew it would cause you to worry."

"That's why you didn't tell me you'd hired someone until after you'd done it."

His dad leveled a stare at him. "In my defense, you were deployed at the time."

Which was true, but the Red Cross had gotten word to the forward operating base which got word to his team. It took almost three weeks, but Gunner had called home as soon as he could. "I know. I'm so sorry I wasn't here to help." That fact ate at Gunner's gut like slow dripping acid.

"Meh, I handled it. I think maybe the fact that there was no one here forced me to get better faster. I placed an advertisement for a bar manager. I interviewed five people. One a day, because anything more than that was too much for me, but I pushed through. At the end of the week, only one candidate meshed with me and, in my opinion, actually knew what the hell they were doing."

Gunner rolled his eyes. "A.J."

"Yep. She opened up the day after I hired her, and we've never looked back. She's a damn good manager. The first day she opened, Delmont swung by to check on the place. He saw her inside, counting money and called for backup since he was off duty. Cops surrounded the place. They stormed the pub, broke the main doors and damaged a window."

"No shit."

His dad grinned. "Yeah, you've met her. Can you imagine? Well, after the dust settled and Delmont healed from his wounds, A.J. went to the mayor, promised she wouldn't sue the city if they repaired all the damage to the pub." His father chuckled. "The Walrus received a brand-new facia. I'd been saving up to replace those doors, but since I didn't need to do that anymore, we took the money and improved the porch, so people can sit outside on nice nights and have a drink without the hubbub of the pub overriding the conversation."

"That was a great idea, Pops." Gunner nodded his head. "I like the idea."

"It was her idea."

Until that.

His dad shrugged and lifted his water glass to his lips. "I know you don't like her..." He took a drink and held up his hand silencing Gunner's response.

Three times in less than twenty-four hours. What was with the people up here not letting him speak?

"She's organized the shift schedule and maximized our profits by cutting out some of the things I let slide. No more freebies to the bartenders' friends, unless its soda. Half-priced drinks are alright, so we at least make costs on the friends' drinks. Some of the old timers didn't like it, but they sucked it up or left. Don't really miss those who did move along."

"Good. I'm sure we can keep those practices going. You realize you don't need her now that I'm home. Give me a month or two to get my feet under me, and I'll be ready to take care of whatever you need." Gunner leaned back as the waitress delivered their drinks. She smiled and batted her lashes at him, but he wasn't in the mood to be impressed. He'd had enough of the female of the species today, thank you very much. He shifted in his seat, still feeling the echoes of pain in his balls. Ghost pain to be sure, but you just don't forget a thing like that. He lifted his drink and took a long pull on it.

His dad took that moment to drop a bomb on his ass. "Son, she's bought into the business. She owns twenty percent."

Gunner swallowed hard, pulling the liquor down without choking or spitting it back up. The expensive drink swirled like sawdust in his mouth. He had no idea his dad had considered selling a portion of the pub. Hell, not that it mattered, the Walrus was his dad's to do with as he saw fit, but if she was part-owner that meant... He glanced over at his dad. "How much time does she spend at the pub?"

"Lives and breathes it, just like I do. Like you will if you're still offering to take it over for me."

Gunner closed his eyes. "Fuck. Me."

"If it is any consolation, she's a nice person. Hell, she made me start exercising. We walk every day. She's got a family back in Texas. She was raised with solid values and morals. She's grounded and a hard worker." His dad took a sip of liquor and a small smile spread across his lips.

Gunner processed the information. "Where do you walk?"

His old man shrugged, "Just around. She stops by, and we head out every day before we come into work. Together. Only had two cars today because I was in San Francisco."

"Wait. Hold on. Where does she live?" Gunner knew the answer before he asked it, but damn it, he needed confirmation anyway.

His dad had a smirk on his face. "Next door to you in the rental property."

"Shit." Gunner took another slug of his drink.

His father chuckled. "I think once you get to know her, you'll like her. I always figured she was the type you liked. Not that I would condone you mixing business and pleasure with the part owner of our business."

Gunner glanced over at his old man and narrowed his eyes. The smirk was firmly fixed on his Pops' face. "She is as far from my type of woman as it gets. My preference for staying dry and undamaged removes her from any consideration."

His dad taunted, "Big bad SEAL afraid of a five-foot-nothing lady?"

Gunner gave a humorless laugh before he responded the jibe, "If you remember correctly, this big bad SEAL was taught by his old man to treat a lady with respect. I can't fight back. Which means I am defenseless. She is not an enemy I can defeat. I'm sticking with the *'do not engage under any circum-stances'* directive."

"Hell son, who said anything about engagements?"

His dad laughed at the middle finger he flipped at him. He was *sooo* glad his father found this situation funny. That old saying, 'a friend of my enemy is my enemy' would fit here. Just whose side was his dad on? His pops was having a bit too much fun with the events of the last twenty-four hours.

a.J. stood at the far end of the bar. It was Friday night, actually Saturday morning, and the place had once again been packed. Lately, the majority of the new clientele tipped the scales heavily toward the female persuasion. The reason was currently standing behind the bar washing glasses. He'd spent the night working and flirting. The bar had been lined two deep with people, mostly women.

Silas had explained that Gunner wanted to get involved in the day-to-day operations. He had jumped in with both feet, but instead of taking on a management role right away, as she assumed he would want to do, he'd asked his father to start him at the bottom of the rung. So, he took the place of the barback they'd fired for stealing. A.J. had watched him for the last three weeks. Gunner Kincade was intense and intelligent. He'd worked hard learning everything that August and Tessa, their two full-time bartenders, taught him. He cleaned, mopped, and stayed diligently attentive behind the bar anticipating what the bartenders needed. He held running conversations with everyone who came in the doors. Both bartenders were comfortable with him pulling drafts, mixing simple cocktails and running the till.

As if a silent pact had been drawn up and signed in blood, A.J. avoided any place that Gunner occupied, and Gunner went out of his way to keep clear of her. She didn't blame him. God, she was still mortified by the coffee fiasco. It took her days to stop seeing his genitals every time she looked at him. Worse, he knew. Her eyes would slip sideways and she'd blush. He'd respond with a look of disgust that she caught in her peripheral vision.

Tonight, she was closing. August had an appointment early in the morning with one of his kids, so he'd left as soon as the crowd started to thin. She watched from her perch at the end of the bar. Gunner handled the bar like he'd been doing it for years. Tonight was the first night he'd break down the bar, do inventory and restock by himself. Unfortunately, the nightly task of balancing the drawer against the new drink tally system was non-negotiable. The bar manager always did it. After closing when everyone else had left and they'd locked up, she would count the till out with him—just the two of them. Perhaps if she stayed seated until he left the pub, she'd avoid doing something catastrophic or utterly inept. She peeked at him from under her lashes from time to time, but he ignored her completely as she sat quietly, pretending to work on her tablet.

He wore a company t-shirt that threatened to shred if the muscles in his arms and chest bulged any further. His beard was fuller now, and she'd seen his unguarded smile a million times as he worked behind the bar. She hated that any chance those smiles would be directed at her was between null and nill. It bothered Silas that they didn't get along. Get along. She mentally snorted. She wouldn't mind being friends with Gunner just so Silas's worries would settle, but every time she closed her eyes, flashes of him ripping that shirt open, or visions of her voyeuristic under-the-towel-episode sprang to mind. Her face heated at the mere thought of his body. In spite of the disastrous repercussions, if she'd been handed a magic wand to wipe out those twenty-four hours, well, she wasn't sure if she would. Gunner Kincade was a little bit like poison. He got under your skin and slowly numbed you to anything else surrounding you. He made her body feel things she shouldn't feel and infected her mind so that he was at the center of the majority of her thoughts. Yeah, he was poison all right, and she'd take it willingly any time he offered. Unfortunately, Gunner had made it perfectly clear that would never happen.

He'd finished the small amount of work he still had behind the bar and opened the till. He hit the tally button, and the electronic device spit out drinks, inventory usage, and money totals. The electronic system tied into the dispensing machines ensuring accurate pours that were charged correctly. It was one of the first things she'd recommended to Silas after she took over management of the bar.

Gunner walked his drawer over along with the documentation. An electronic copy would also be sent to the new inventory system that had just been installed so A.J. could disperse the records to the accountant and have them on a moment's notice if they were ever inspected. He set the drawer down and turned on his heel without a word.

"When are you going to stop punishing me for making a mistake?" A.J. asked as she arranged the tape he'd brought over.

A humorless laugh drifted over to her. "A mistake?"

That question wasn't fair. She lifted her head to look at him and was surprised that he was actually making eye contact with her. "Yes, a mistake. Kicking you in the...kicking you was a mistake. One I apologized for many, many times." She put her pen down. He'd never actually accepted any of her attempted apologies. Something else that bothered her. She'd been raised to forgive those who hurt her if they were truly sorry. She shook her head with a small motion and finished almost to herself, "Everything else was a series of..." she blew a long breath out, "...I don't know, mishaps or unfortunate happenings."

"Are you always so accident prone?" Gunner

leaned against the back of the bar with his arms crossed over his chest, his legs crossed at the ankles, appearing nothing short of masculine perfection. A.J. blinked at him. *What had he said?* Oh. "No. I guess you bring out that specific trait."

He cocked his head and stared at her. "Why did you move to Half Moon Bay?"

Gunner didn't change position, but the tone of his voice changed. It didn't seem as cold. Maybe that was wishful thinking, but it was the most they'd talked to each other since "that" day. "My ex had a problem dealing with the fact that I broke up with him." She lowered her eyes. The bastard had almost killed her before she'd been able to grab a liquor bottle and break it over his head. She'd been able to crawl to the phone and call the cops before he regained consciousness. "He's currently serving fifteen years in the Texas State Penn for attempted murder."

Gunner's eyes snapped up to hers. "Wait, he tried to kill you?"

She nodded. If only that was the end of the story.

"I'm sorry that happened to you. So, you moved here looking for a fresh start?"

A.J. glanced at him trying to judge the sincerity of his comment. He hadn't moved, but she couldn't detect any mockery.

She decided to tell him the truth. "My ex has a checkered past. His near and extended family has been in and out of the state penitentiary for a variety of crimes—assault, armed robbery, and his oldest brother was convicted of stalking. My family and friends warned me not to get involved with him, but..." She chuckled but it wasn't funny, it was sad. So damn sad. She should have listened, but at the time, she thought she loved Marcus. "After he was arrested, his brothers tried to intimidate me. They never crossed the line that would allow me to charge them for harassment or stalking, but for months his older brothers followed me. They showed up where I was, taunted and threatened me when there were no witnesses. The night they cornered me and suggested I kill myself, so they didn't have to do it, I broke." She glanced over at him and shrugged. "If I stayed, I have no doubt they would have driven me insane or killed me." She wiped at a tear that threatened to fall. "Or they might have gone after my sisters. There were insinuations, never outright threats, but enough that I worried. I knew it was only a matter of time before they did something. So, I loaded up my car, said goodbye to my family and in the dark of night I pulled out of town heading west. I worked my way here. Spent a couple months in five or six different bars working as a bartender. Once as an assistant manager. I managed the largest bar in our town. Well until Marcus tried to kill me there. I lost my job because he was inside the bar after closing. Against company policy. Never mind that he broke in." She shook her head trying to dislodge the thoughts. Taking a firm grip on herself, she continued, "Anyway, I saw the ad your dad put in the paper and answered it. And presto, you have my story in three minutes or less."

She left out the fact that Marcus's brothers had shown up at the first two places she'd found work. She didn't look at Gunner, busying herself instead with counting out the drawer. She'd told Silas her story before he'd hired her. If Marcus's family followed her...well, Gunner deserved to know she had a past and it wasn't pretty, but he didn't need to know everything.

"Is that the reason you freaked out when I laughed and walked up the stairs?" The closeness of his voice spooked her. She jumped as she swept her eyes up to him.

She opened her mouth to say yes but couldn't. She shook her head. "I don't know. Do I still look over my shoulder? Yes, but it is getting less frequent. My past still haunts me. Is that the reason I kicked you? I don't honestly know. Maybe is the best answer I can give."

His dark brown eyes held hers for a long moment before he nodded once and put his hands on the bar on either side of the cash drawer. "If you ever see those bastards, or even think you might have, you let me know. You never have to worry about them again."

Her brow furrowed in confusion. "Why would you do that? I figure I'm pretty much nothing to you."

"It's true we got off on the wrong foot, but you're important to my pops, and you're good for him and the Walrus. All that makes you something to me." Gunner spun and went through the process of locking up the bar. She smiled as she looked down at the cash drawer. It was flimsy, but it felt like an olive branch. She'd take it.

CHAPTER 6

*G*unner lengthened his stride as he rounded the curve about a mile from the house. He'd run the circuit he'd mapped out twice today. Things were actually looking up. He was learning his dad's business from the ground up. Sweeping, mopping and cleaning wasn't his idea of taking over a business, but he did know in order to be successful at anything you started with the basics, and there was no way he'd ever walk in assuming he knew how to run the Walrus.

His feet hit the pavement with the same, steady, consistent stride. The motion and repetition were soothing, and the lack of any cars or hazards on the road allowed him to think. His conversation last night with A.J. was...enlightening. He was simultaneously furious that anyone would lay a hand on her, or any woman, in anger, and happy that she'd been open enough to tell him the truth. The anger at her situation was the reason he'd extended his run this morning. Well, that and the fact she thought she was nothing to him. Fuck, he'd avoided her initially because of the walking disaster mode she'd perpetuated, but over the last three weeks, he'd observed her —from a distance, because his safety was a paramount concern around the woman. It would appear the 'normal' mode for A.J. Ericson was professional, efficient, friendly, and sexy in a confident, understated way. Her clothes weren't too tight or too revealing, yet there was no denying her banging hot body. At work, the woman wore four-inch heels. A smile spread across his face. She was a firecracker and took absolutely zero shit from anyone, customer or staff, yet she was a complete professional. Her dark auburn hair was always pulled back into a thick ponytail, and he'd felt those expressive green eyes track him when they worked the same shifts.

Somehow, he always knew where she was when she was in the pub. At first, he could chalk it up to self-preservation, but as the days flowed into weeks, he acknowledged it was because she intrigued and attracted him. Which was hard to admit. He did not want to like the woman, but he did. Respected her even. The conversation last night had acted like a fissure to the surface for his repressed emotions, allowing his feelings to bubble toward the surface. Elements of desire were present. Since the night he walked out of the water and saw her standing by Delmont he'd desired her. His need to protect her from those who had hurt her in the past had also seeped out, and that was dangerous. Desire by itself was something he knew how to handle. He was the self-anointed king of no-strings relationships. Those urges to put her in a safe place and guard the door? That was going to get his ass in some serious trouble.

He rounded the corner on the final stretch about a half mile from his house and poured out all the energy that he had left, sprinting at a full out run. The world narrowed to his breathing and pace, all thoughts and worries disappeared as the most basic functions took over. A runner's high. He reined in his pace as he passed his house. His lungs and legs burned but in a good way. Walking to normalize his heart and breathing he passed the house A.J. rented and walked down the small access road. He stutter-stepped when he saw her standing on the edge of the beach, but mindful of the new and tenuous truce they'd called, he continued.

She turned her head when he approached. The shy smile she gave him was new, and he liked it. "Good morning."

She glanced at her watch. "Good afternoon."

He chuckled. "I must have run longer than I thought." He put his hands on his hips and considered his next words carefully before he spoke, "Thank you for telling me about your past. I know it couldn't have been easy."

She shrugged and turned away. "Marcus was one of the worst mistakes of my life."

Gunner glanced at her. "One of the worst?" He tried for levity, "There's more?"

She gave a dry laugh and nodded. "Yeah, once upon a time I kicked this guy in the balls. Found out after the fact he was a pretty decent person. It ruined my chances of getting to know him."

He stood beside her and gazed out on the water, not knowing how to respond to that comment. It was calm and cool today, which was the weather fifty percent of the time in Half Moon Bay. The other fifty percent fog, rain, and even cooler temperatures battled for dominance. In the distance, he saw a boat cutting through the waves of the unprotected water. She turned to go back toward the houses. He stopped her with his words, "You didn't ruin your chances. I'm pretty sure that guy has forgiven you."

She cocked her head at him and asked, "Pretty sure?"

"Yeah, you may have to grovel a bit, but I think it's a given he'll forgive you."

"Grovel?"

Gunner nodded and rubbed the back of his neck. "Yeah, I hear a home cooked meal goes a long way in the groveling department." His father had told him about the cakes and cookies she sometimes brought into the Walrus. If the woman could cook? Getting an invite to dinner was a stretch, but hey, in for a penny, in for a pound.

Her smile lit up her face. "Well, if you see that guy, tell him to come by for dinner on Sunday night."

She started walking back up the hill when he called out to her. "What time should I tell him to be there?"

"Tell him to come at seven." She didn't turn around, but he could hear the amusement in her voice.

He walked the shoreline and then headed up to his own house. He took off his shoes in the garage, placing them on the rack just inside the door of the kitchen as he entered. His clothes landed in a heap inside the laundry basket on his way to the shower. He cranked the knobs and waited for the water to warm. He gazed at himself in the mirror and mentally groaned. He leaned closer. *Fuck.* There was a grey hair in his beard. Just one, but it was there. Didn't that just make him feel old as fuck? At forty, his body was still in good condition. The training he did on a daily basis kept him fit, although he'd scaled his workouts down from the rigors of day-to-day training in Coronado. Granted, he wasn't as fast as he used to be, and it took longer in the morning to loosen up after a hard workout then it did when he was younger, but didn't that commercial say forty was the new thirty? *Get over yourself, Kincade.* He snagged the offending grey hair between his thumb and index finger and yanked. His eyes watered. *Holy shit-balls.* He regretted the decision immediately. *Fuck, that hurt.*

The steam from the shower finally started to crawl over the glass doors calling him into the warmth. The run had relaxed him, and the conversation with A.J. had gone better than he had a right to hope. Talking without bodily injury or incidental exposure was an improvement. Well...a rueful chuckle echoed in the confines of the glass-enclosed shower. No more denial about his attraction to her. Not any longer. A.J. walloped every one of his ideal woman requirements with a one-two punch.

Gunner ignored the urge to reach down and rub one out while thinking about all the boxes that woman ticked. Instead, he showered quickly and got out. He may be old-fashioned, or hella stupid, but considering the things he'd recently learned about her, he figured she deserved someone who would respect her. Maybe he'd get a shot at being that man. A wicked grin spread across his face. As a matter of fact, he'd make it his objective to be that man. Target acquired.

CHAPTER 7

A.J. had witnessed Gunner's charm as he worked the crowd from behind the bar, but she'd never had the full force of it turned on her. This week had been insanely busy. Tessa had called in sick, so A.J. stepped up and pulled Tessa's scheduled shifts. At first, she'd thought she'd imagined the attention... the small touches that seemed to come out of nowhere and last for only moments. As if reading her mind, Gunner's hand rested lightly on her back as he walked behind her at the bar, letting her know he was crossing. She glanced up from the blender drink she was making, and he winked at her. A.J. felt the fire in her cheeks.

A gorgeous brunette leaned against the bar. A.J. poured the strawberry daiquiri, added whipped cream and a split strawberry to the top. She handed it to the woman who had ordered it, added the cost to the woman's tab and turned her attention to the new arrival. "What can I get you?" A.J. wiped the bar in front of the woman and slipped a paper coaster with the Walrus' logo on it in front of her.

"I'll take him." The woman's attention was focused down the bar where Gunner poured draft beer for an order he'd taken.

"Sorry, don't think he's on the menu. Do you actually want a drink?" A.J. held on tightly to the grip she had on her fake smile. The woman's interest in Gunner nudged emotions she didn't want to admit to feeling.

"Whoa, a little hostility there?" The woman drew her eyes from Gunner and gave A.J. an obvious once-over and immediate dismissal as if she wasn't even to be considered as competition.

"I'm sorry if you thought so, we *are* very busy. Please place your order or move, so the people behind you can be served." A.J. placed her hands on her hips. It was something she did to take up just a little more space. Being small-statured her entire life, she'd learned how to stand up for herself, be a little bit louder than most, and not back down when she knew she was right. It had worked for the most part, until Marcus.

"Fine, I'll have some sex on the beach." The woman's voice softened to a purr as she spoke.

A hand on her back preceded Gunner leaning into her. He bent down and spoke to her so no one else could hear, "Are you all right? You look upset."

She glanced up at him. The concern in his voice

was echoed in his eyes. She gave him a tight smile and shook her head before she whispered, "The customer is being difficult. Nothing I can't handle."

Gunner kept his head lowered but glanced at the woman who preened under his darted look. He turned his gaze back down to her and smiled before he winked. "You've got this."

Before A.J. could reply he dropped a kiss to her forehead and headed back down to take care of those who wanted a draft beer or bottled beer. A.J. stood there transfixed as she watched him leave.

"Can I get my drink?" The woman's voice snapped A.J. back to reality.

"Sure, you wanted sex on the beach." She grabbed a cocktail shaker and the vodka looking for the peach schnapps.

"No, just give me a Chardonnay."

A.J. glanced up at the woman and shrugged. "No problem, whatever you want."

The woman glanced down the bar. "Evidently not."

A.J. placed the wine on the bar. "Will that be all or are you opening a tab?"

"Since it appears you aren't serving what I originally ordered..." the woman dropped a ten, "...No need to stay." She turned and walked away.

A.J. spun and rang up the drink, deposited the ten and drew the change out of the register, throwing it into the tip jar that she'd split between Gunner and Tessa at the end of the night. Tessa needed the tips more than she ever would, and A.J. wasn't going to deny her a portion of her income because she was sick.

The kiss on the forehead had unsettled her. Her hands shook. For the rest of the night, each time she'd get lost in the grind of work, a touch, caress, whisper or wink would intrude and nosedive her down the fluttery butterfly rabbit-hole her mind told her to avoid. Too bad her heart hadn't gotten the message. Gunner Kincade angry and avoiding her she could handle, but Gunner Kincade focused, attentive, flirtatious and protective? There was a beast that could easily consume her. She'd let him overwhelm her without a fight. Lord have mercy, she wanted his touches. She coveted them. She thirsted for his attention and ached to have him care enough about her to be protective.

She poured two martinis, added the extra olives that were requested and set the drinks down in front of the two regulars who had a running tab. She spun to log the orders and slammed into a brick wall. Hands grabbed her arms keeping her from reeling backward.

"Sorry, babe." Gunner released her. He winked as he passed by her heading to the cooler.

"Babe?" She whispered the word as she charged the drinks and slipped the receipt into the appropriate folio. A.J. glanced back at Gunner. He was laughing with several couples as he popped beer bottle caps and set the open bottles in front of the customers. He collected the cash and headed back to the till. She surveyed the bar and then glanced at the clock. The crowd was thinning, and nobody seemed to need a drink refreshed at the moment.

She shuffled to the left so Gunner could ring up the last purchase. He dropped the change into the tip jar and jammed the bills down, so they didn't over-flow. The crowd had been generous tonight. He shut the till, and spun, leaning on the back shelves. He nodded at the front of the house. "A good night for the most part. I need to go bus the front of the house. You got this?"

A.J. nodded. He grabbed a plastic bin and headed out to collect their customers' evening detritus. The 'babe' comment *had* to be a slip of the tongue. There was no way it was a term of endearment. She scrubbed that flickering fantasy out of her mind and got busy. There was always something to do behind the bar. The hot soapy water called her, so she headed over and made short work of washing and sanitizing the glasses that were stacked to the side of the station. As she rinsed the last glass, she caught the eye of the brunette who had stayed after all, and her one glass of Chardonnay had turned into three. The brunette directed a taunting smile at her before she spun and sidled up to Gunner where he worked clearing a table. Blood red fingertips trailed up his bicep, and the woman leaned toward him. The invi-tation was obvious. Gunner smiled at her and A.J. dropped her eyes. She didn't want to witness her feeble imagined chances with Gunner vaporize like the apparition it appeared to be. Call it self-preservation. She didn't have to watch this spider catch that fly.

A request for another drink was a welcome distraction. A.J. chastised herself for entertaining such stupid romantic dreams. She made the requested Jack and Coke and drew a deep breath. She needed to pull her head out of the clouds and face the fact Gunner Kincade had not singled her out for special treatment. He treated everyone the way he'd been treating her tonight. She'd make him dinner on Sunday night. They'd have a polite conversation, and she'd go to bed. Alone. Again. Which was fine with her. Men complicated things and were risks to one's physical health. Part of her immediately objected. *Not him, he isn't like Marcus.* Great. Just what she needed, a duel with her own brain. No, Gunner was nothing like Marcus, but he was a complication. She came here to put down roots. To find a place away from the drama of her east Texas home and to be happy. *Doesn't being happy mean finding a man to share your life with?* A.J. growled and quickly glanced around to make sure no one had heard her. Satisfied no one was paying attention to the mental debate raging in her head, she shoved back at the thought. No, she didn't have to find a man. She was just fine as she was. Period. End of story. *I am woman, hear me roar.* A.J. snorted and shook her head. "Rawr," she snickered. Two more asked for their tab, interrupting her rousing back-and-forth with herself. She busied herself closing out accounts and cleaning behind the bar. Gunner was nowhere to be seen, which was okay. He hadn't had a break all night. It would have been nice of him to tell her he was stepping out, but whatever. A.J. closed out the last tab and called the local cab to come to get one of her regulars after a lively but short-lived argument with the obviously drunk man. She wasn't going to lose their liquor license because someone got behind the wheel incapacitated. It was worth the seventeen dollars the cabbie would charge. She'd deliver Bartlett to the curb along with a soda for the cabbie and then lock the door and put an end to one of the longest nights she'd endured since she took the job. Lord above, her feet ached. If she'd walked an inch, she'd walked five miles. She grabbed the elastic of her bra and adjusted it. The melted daiquiri that a regular had tipped over and splashed her with had long since dried into a distant memory. The stickiness? Not so much. She made a mental note to replenish the hand cream under the bar. Her hands were pruned and chapped from washing and sanitizing an evening's worth of drink glasses. The minutia of the end of shift matters hadn't been important earlier tonight, but now with her ridiculous dreams smashed at her feet, the details were needed to fill the void that seemed to have opened inside her soul. She cast her glance toward the front of the house. It was time to go home. Past time, actually.

A loud thud resounded behind her. She gave a startled gasp and jumped two feet. Okay, probably not two feet, but dammit, the noise had startled her. Gunner lifted a keg of beer from the stack of three on the wheeled cart.

"Is that where you've been? Getting fresh kegs?" her voice squeaked. She cleared her throat and observed Bartlett falling asleep in the booth by the door.

"Roger that, and I took out the trash. Why? Was there a problem?" His glance cut through almost deserted pub, instantly tense.

She shook her head. "No. No problem. I just didn't realize you'd gone to get beer. I assumed you'd walked that woman to her car."

A puzzled expression splashed across his face. "What woman?"

A.J. gave a bitter laugh. "Right, what woman." She watched headlights turn onto Main Street. The cab pulled up outside, and A.J. moved to wake Bartlett.

Gunner's hand stilled her. "I was serious. What woman?"

"The brunette." She nodded her head toward the table where the woman had pawed possessively at him, and then stepped around Gunner and gathered Bartlett. He swayed but stood on his own which allowed A.J. to grab the can of soda she'd put on the table. It took some gentle guidance, but Bartlett found his way into the back seat of the cab. A.J. handed the driver a twenty and the soda. The cabby honked once as he pulled away from the front of the Walrus, and A.J. gave him a quick wave.

A local police car cruised by and the driver slowed to a stop. The window descended and Gary Herman inquired, "Quiet night tonight, A.J.?"

"Yep, everyone's gone. We're closing up." She enjoyed the novelty of a friendly police officer. Especially after the way her tenure at the Walrus started. Well...at least the entire police force for Half Moon Bay now knew what she looked like—so that was good.

"You and Tessa tonight?"

A.J. shook her head. "Tessa called out. I'm with Gunner tonight. Silas's son."

"Tessa's sick?"

A.J. smiled at the concern that was clearly displayed across the young officer's face. "Yeah, she thinks she has that stomach flu that has been going around."

Gary nodded. "You need me to wait and take you to your car?"

"No, thanks, Gunner will be here to walk me out."

"Alright. Night A.J."

"Night." She smiled at the budding romance and wondered if she'd ever be so lucky. Tessa and that young officer were a cute couple. She waited until the patrol car turned off the main road before she headed into the silent bar. Out of habit she threw the deadbolt, set the alarm and turned off the open sign before she made her way back behind the bar. The kegs had been changed out, and the dolly carrying them was no longer behind the bar.

The slam of the storage room door confirmed Gunner had taken the empties back to await the manufacturer's retrieval. She grabbed the bleach water pail and started wiping down the front of the house. She heard Gunner sweeping as she scrubbed down the tables and chairs. After she thoroughly cleaned each chair, she lifted them seat down on top of the tables. When she was done, she went to the storage closet and filled the mop bucket. The same one she'd used to drown Gunner that horrible morning weeks ago. Concentrating on the steady stream of water flowing into the pail she let herself relive that humiliation.

"We need to talk."

Startled, she spun, losing control of the bucket. It fell to the floor and tipped sending at least two gallons of water over her feet and his. She screeched, "Don't do that!"

Gunner stood with his arms out from his sides staring at his soaked boots. Her gut dropped, and if there was ever a time in her life when she wished the ground would part and swallow her from sight, this was it. Instead, she apologized, again. "I'm sorry. God, I didn't mean to do that." She might have whined that last comment.

She reached down in an attempt to snatch the bucket. Unfortunately, it coincided with Gunner doing the same thing. Shooting pain stabbed her head at the same time as the echo of the collision radiated through her brain. She hissed and grabbed her head.

"Fuck!"

His roar echoed her thoughts. A.J. dropped to her butt. The wet floor be damned.

"Are you all right? Hey, look at me."

A.J. shook her head, keeping her hands pressed firmly over the knot that was forming on the top of her head.

"Come on, sweetheart. I need to take a look at your eyes and make sure you don't have a concussion."

"Stop. Just stop that, okay?" She yelled the words with her eyes clenched shut. Tears of frustration and pain pushed through her lashes.

"I'm not doing anything." His voice was soft and full of concern. His warm arm pressed into hers as he sat on the floor beside her.

She couldn't do this. A.J. opened her eyes and blinked bringing him into focus. "Stop calling me babe and sweetheart. It isn't fair. You can't flirt with me and then go out with other women. I'm not that kind of person. Just go. Leave me alone. I'll clean this up. I just can't play that kind of game." She closed her eyes and buried her face in her hands.

"Hey, come here." His words no sooner registered than she was slid up onto his lap. She tensed in his hold. He pulled her into his chest until he rested his chin over her head.

"I'm wet, I'll ruin your jeans." She was soaked actually and tired and upset and just...over it.

"Hmmm...it would seem that I'm wet too. Sitting in mop water tends to do that, but I have a change of clothes in Dad's office, so stop worrying about me. I told you we needed to talk. I did not walk that woman out to her car. I didn't want to. Was the invitation there? Oh hell yes, but she isn't who I want to go home with." His chest rumbled under her ear as he spoke.

A.J. sniffed and wiped her cheeks. "I'm sure you have your pick of the line-up." She tried to move away from him, but he wrapped his arms around her and prevented her from leaving.

"You're probably right, but that doesn't matter. The only person I'm interested in is currently sitting on my lap in a room flooded with soapy water."

A.J. tipped her head back and he moved so their eyes could meet. "Me?" Her voice sounded small and unsure even to her own ears.

"You."

A.J. gasped as he lowered and covered her lips with his. She slipped her arms up and around his neck. His hands splayed across her back as he pulled her into his kiss. His tongue licked the seam of her lips. She sighed and opened for him, overwhelmed by the tenderness of his approach.

She shifted and ran her fingers through his hair as he consumed the physical space around them. Everything but his possession of her lips and their embrace ceased to exist. He lifted his head trailing kisses across her cheek and before he spoke, "Look at me."

"No." She didn't want to look at him.

His chest vibrated, and the rumble of laughter surrounded her. He squeezed her gently. "Why not?"

"Because I'm afraid if I open my eyes you wouldn't be there. That this moment isn't real. That maybe I knocked myself unconscious, and I'm dreaming."

"I'm not positive, but I don't think you dream when you're unconscious." Another light kiss dropped to her lips.

"How do you know? Have you ever been unconscious?" She kept her eyes closed and sighed.

"Once or twice." The teasing tone of his voice didn't change.

She popped her eyes open and stared at him. "I'm sorry."

He blinked and shook his head. "For what?"

"For braining you just now, and for assuming you were interested in that woman. I thought with the touches and when you called me babe...and then when she had her hands all over you...that smile you gave her..."

"That smile happened two seconds before I told her point blank that I wasn't interested in anyone except the cute redhead behind the bar—the one in a strange relationship with mop water." He traced her nose with his index finger before dropping it to her lips. "Just kidding. I was attracted to you the moment I saw you illuminated by the patrol car's headlights.

We just need to work on this ninja-stealth-mode-assassination-fascination you have going on."

"I'm really not a klutz." She leaned her head against his chest and laughed. "I'm actually quite graceful."

He threw back his head and laughed. His chest moved under her head as his mirth filled the small storage room. "I can absolutely tell. You're as graceful as a swan. Come on, I'll help you get rid of the evidence to the contrary before I change."

"Why do you have a change of clothes here?" A.J. groaned as she lifted to her feet. Her head hurt, the backside of her jeans were drenched. He looked at her and raised an eyebrow. "Oh." She felt her face flame again. His laughter echoed around her. They both grabbed mops and he righted the bucket. She sloshed the soaked mop into the mop bucket's wringer attachment and squeezed the water out of the mop. She glanced at him out of the corner of her eye. The night had been screwed up, well at least for her. On the plus side, Gunner had kissed her, several times. Based on recent history with the man, she'd consider that a win.

CHAPTER 8

*G*unner put his truck in park, turned it off and headed out seconds after he pushed the remote access button to close the garage door. On the pretense that it was the gentlemanly thing to do, he headed over to A.J.'s house to make sure she got inside safely. He scooted inside the garage just as she opened the door of her small car. Her smile lit up his insides.

"Hello, sailor. Come here often?"

He watched as she made sure to pull the handful of bar towels she'd covered her seat with off before she shut the door. He shook his head when she looked back up at him. "No, ma'am. My first time. I'm in foreign territory."

Her eyes widened coyishly as she pushed the button to close the garage door. "Well, we need to ensure you get the lay of the land. We wouldn't want you off course, now would we?"

KRIS MICHAELS

He pulled her into him and palmed both hands over her tight little ass. The wet denim did nothing to distract him from his objective for the evening. He straightened, lifting her into his arms. She squeaked and scrambled, wrapping her arms securely behind his neck. He growled and nuzzled into her neck. "Wrap your legs around me."

She tipped her head back and laughed as she did what he asked. "If I'm dreaming, for the love of everything good, don't wake me up." She lifted her head and found his eyes. "Don't ever wake me up."

"You're not dreaming." He lifted her a bit higher and grabbed her ass with one hand, opening the kitchen door with the other. He knew the layout of the rental. Growing up, he'd cleaned it for extra allowance money when renters moved out. Her lips caressed then sucked the area just behind and below his ear. Fuck, her touch ignited a passion-filled lust that had been burning uncontrolled just under his skin since he'd realized she wasn't actually trying to kill him. He kicked the door shut and made quick work of attaining his goal, the master bedroom, while her lips and tongue stoked that blaze. Every small touch or kiss poured gallons of kerosene onto an intense, growing fire.

He bounced off the door frame, kissing her and trying to see at the same time. The kiss won. With her in his arms, he stood in the middle of the room, lost in the dance of their tongues.

She pulled away biting his bottom lip as she withdrew. "Having problems finding the bed, sailor?" Her hands pulled at his t-shirt, but it was trapped under the tight grip of her thighs.

"No, ma'am." He looked over his shoulder before he waggled his eyebrows, lifted her away from him and tossed her onto the bed.

He moved to follow her, but she sat up and turned on a small bedside lamp. "Whoa, there big guy."

He stopped halfway down to her and teased, "Oh God, please don't say no. I'll go home, but my balls will be blue for a week. Don't they deserve a little kindness?"

She chuckled softly. "We'll get there, but first I want to see that chest again, and this time I want to enjoy it." She sat on her heels in her wet jeans.

"Only if I get to see you, too." A wolfish smile split his face.

She pinched her chin between her thumb and forefinger and hummed as if considering it. "All right. You take off your shirt, and I'll take off mine."

His t-shirt whipped through the air and landed somewhere to his right. She reached down and undulated as she slowly teased the hem of her shirt up revealing flawless white skin. Already awake and plenty happy, he could now use his cock as a crowbar and it would forever sport the indelible teeth marks of his zipper. Her lacey black bra barely covered her breasts. The white of her skin held a rose hue which grew darker as he examined every inch of her gloriously bared torso.

"You're next."

He'd never heard more welcome words. He lost his boots and socks. A.J. unzipped her boots and peeled them off. Little black socks joined the pile of clothes. Gunner popped the button on his jeans. His cock jumped in delight. He was very careful when he unzipped making sure the damn thing didn't catch on the boxer briefs pushed against the metal teeth. His cock pushed a tent in the front of his boxers.

A.J. lay down on the bed and unfastened her button and zipper. She grabbed the headboard and lifted a foot toward him. "Pull."

There was no way she'd have to ask twice. He grabbed the hem of both legs and yanked. The denim resisted, but he tugged again and won the battle. He gazed down at her. A band of lace held the smallest triangle of material barely covering her mons Veneris —he knew that Latin class would come in handy sooner or later. He lowered to a knee between her spread legs intent on one thing. He glanced up one more time to make sure A.J. was on the same page.

She reached down and ran her hands through his hair. "I want to know what that beard feels like."

Green light. Gunner dipped his head and kissed her hip, trailing his tongue to the lace. Her fingers stayed in his hair, and her legs fell open. He was in fucking Nirvana. Both hands worked the thong down her hips and thighs. He moved so she could kick the lace off. His gaze traveled over her. She was beautiful. He started trailing kisses from her hip to her belly button, giving tiny nips that he soothed with more kisses. He traveled up her rib cage and nestled teasing kisses and licks just under the lace of her bra. Her back arched, pushing her flesh into his mouth. He took the opportunity to reach under her and unsnap the offending garment. He nosed the material out of his way as his fingers reversed course and traveled south. She bucked against his fingers when he found her core and moaned when he started to work her slickness back and forth across her engorged nub while he suckled on her rose-colored nipple. He could devour the woman, consume her and then do it again. When he slowed, she demanded more. When he played, she scolded. As he built her desire, she dug her fingers into his back and bit his shoulder.

"Please, don't stop."

As if that was an option. A.J. moaned deliciously when he moved lower and centered himself between her legs. She opened like a flower, ripe for his taking and take her is exactly what he did. As he ran his tongue over her heated skin, her hips bucked up wildly. He wrapped his arms around her legs and held her still. This beautiful, sweet, warm and delicious woman deserved to know ecstasy, and he was going to take her there. He couldn't stop. He worked her body with his mouth and fingers until she tensed.

Her hands fisted in his hair. "*Oh...there...yes...yes...Ahhh!*" Her body clenched, tightening in a rhythmic pulse against his fingers.

Gunner loved the fuck out of her uncensored responses. He wanted more of A.J., more of both of them on the same page, in the same bed, working together, more than just this evening. He wanted more and more wasn't something he'd ever considered with any other woman.

He lifted away from her delicate skin. She grabbed at his arm. "Where are you going?"

"Nowhere." He dropped his boxers, and his cock slapped his stomach. He could use the damn thing to pound nails. "Oh my God! It is a good thing I don't have a bone left in my body. You're huge!"

Gunner threw back his head and laughed before he leaned over kissed her soundly on the lips. When he pulled away, he growled, "My ego thanks you." He waggled his eyebrows at her and moved to grab his jeans. He had two condoms tucked inside his wallet. Only two, and somehow, he didn't think that would be sufficient for what he wanted to do with this woman.

"The free ogle I got that first day didn't do you justice." She lifted up onto her elbows and ran her eyes over him. He tossed the condoms onto the bed and crawled back over her. She surprised him when she pushed him back and to the side. He went with it and fell onto the bed. "On your back. I want to show you why us girls from Texas are so famous."

"Really? Texas girls have a claim to fame?" He moved onto his back as she straddled him.

"Oh yes, haven't you heard?" She leaned down and kissed him before she lifted away running her nails down his chest. She ignited every sensory receptor in his body which, at this moment, funneled straight to his cock, and that dude didn't need encouragement. He watched her reach for and open the condom wrapper. Turning back to him with an innocent expression, she batted her lashes as she spoke, "Texas women make the best cowgirls in the world." Her hand circled the base of his cock, and with her other hand, she rolled a condom onto him. "'cause we all just *love* to ride."

"Shit, your hands feel so good." There was no doubt he'd spill in her hand if she continued to stroke him like that. He grabbed her and moved her up his body before he grabbed his cock. He encircled the base in a tight grip to push back the orgasm looming far too closely. She trailed kisses over his shoulders as he pulled himself back from the edge. Moment of crisis past, he settled his hand at her hip. "Hmmm...I think I'm ready for some proof of this famous talent. Show me whatcha got cowgirl. Make Texas proud."

A.J. smiled and pulled her hair out of the haphazard ponytail, sending her auburn hair tumbling to her shoulders. With a wicked grin, she reached back through her legs centered his shaft between her soft, slick folds, and sank down at the rate of one millimeter per hour. Gunner closed his eyes and moaned as her tight heat surrounded him quarter-inch by quarter-inch until the weight of her body rested on his hips. It took fucking hours. Probably. The clock might call him a liar, but he knew what he knew. Fucking hours. It was ecstasy and agony.

God, he wanted to see this. His eyes flew open. A.J.'s back arched, her hands barely rested on his pecs as she lifted her hips and lowered them. Her hips swiveled and undulated with each slow drag of her tight, hot, slick, flesh up and down his hyper-sensitive shaft. As much as he wanted to watch, his eyes crossed from the leisurely torture by pleasure. He forced them back open. His hands found purchase, not to stop her, God no, but to anchor himself from levitating off the bed.

Beautiful didn't describe the woman who'd mounted him and was currently writhing on his cock. Her chest and face blushed with a light rose hue. Her lithe body presented a visual feast, and the look in her eyes as she gazed down at him filled him with stupid, reckless thoughts. Thoughts of relationships and permanence skidded through his mind. The imminent orgasm burning at the base of his spine chased them away.

A.J.'s pace stuttered, and Gunner seized the moment. He flipped them and nestled between her legs. Wrapping his arms underneath her and cupping her shoulders, he clutched against his chest while his hips found the rhythm he needed. He shifted to get deeper and earned a low approving hum from A.J. He thrust a little bit harder. She gasped and clutched his ass to her tightly. Yeah, that was all he needed to know. Finding his own release had been his intention but taking her to the edge with him was now firmly his goal.

Her mouth found his neck and bit before she sucked the sting away. Basic instinct drove him forward. Her legs wrapped around him and she sank her heels into the back of his thighs. He sucked in air in short pants as his hips plunged into her heat again and again. A.J. released his ass and gasped, "Yes!"

Her hot flesh tightened on his cock and she cried out his name. At that point, nothing in the world could have prevented his release. He cradled her in his arms as his orgasm detonated. His body moved as explosions of light flared behind his eyelids. He sucked air only when he realized he'd been holding his breath. It was damn near everything he could do to keep from dropping on top of A.J. and smothering her. He carefully withdrew and dropped at her side. He took care of the condom and then pulled her into him.

"That was amazing." She ran her hand up his arm as she spoke.

The action sent a shiver through him, the aftershocks from one hellacious earthquake of an orgasm. "I'll second that." He pushed her hair away from her face and leaned in to kiss her. "You were right. Texas girls have a great talent."

She laughed. "Right? I'm surprised it's not a

better-known fact, but hey, I'm glad to be the one to educate you."

He trailed a finger across her collarbone. God, he hoped like hell things got easier between them. If shit got awkward now, he'd be royally fucked, because he wanted to see where things between them could go. What if she didn't want the same thing? What would he do? How would he be able to work with her? Hell, he lived two hundred yards from her. He closed his eyes and shook his head to clear all the doubts away. Shit, he didn't like the questions, the worry. They were foreign, unexpected and unwelcome. Now wasn't the time for any type of deep introspection, but regardless, the questions were there. "What do we do now?" His thoughts escaped as a whispered question.

She drew a deep breath and then lifted one delicate shoulder in a shrug. "I have some ideas." She lifted eyes filled with warmth and humor to him. "We'll figure it out. If our history is any indication, we'll mess up plenty. Probably ought to increase your health insurance."

"As long as we can make up like that, I'll wade through all the misunderstandings and personal injury." Gunner moved in for another kiss.

CHAPTER 9

*G*unner shut A.J.'s front door and headed back to his house. The sun had long since crested in the east. He glanced at his watch and smiled. They'd fallen into an exhausted sleep at about five this morning. It was now ten o'clock, and he was dragging his happy ass home. He needed to shower, make a drugstore run for condoms, and then he had another shift with A.J. tonight. He tossed his keys up into the air and caught them with a laugh.

"Well, look what the cat is dragging home." Silas leaned against his front door, dressed and ready to go for his daily walk. With A.J. *Well that could be awkward.*

Gunner stopped and did a three sixty. He held up his hands. "I don't see a cat."

"You're an adult, so is she. Just make sure you don't mess up the business end of the situation, and I'll have no dog in this fight." Silas came down the front steps and motioned toward Gunner's house. Both men sauntered in that direction.

Echoes of his thoughts last night bounced through his mind. "I thought we were talking about cats?"

"You know what I mean, boy. Don't get smart with me." He swatted the back of Gunner's head catching only a bit of hair. A signature move of his dad's. "Upstart kid."

"Hey, just taking after my old man." Gunner laughed at his pops.

"Yeah, such a shame. Anyway, she's a good woman and you, hell, you know I love you. I think you two fit together well. In my mind, you make sense. But if it doesn't work out between you, we still have a business to run." Silas leaned against the railing of the front stoop of Gunner's house.

"She's...different..." Gunner leaned against the opposite rail from his father. "And when she's not trying to have me arrested, or drowning me in dirty mop water, she's pretty fucking amazing." A smile spread across his face.

"See, that is what I always knew. The woman is fantastic. If I were twenty years younger..." Silas winked at him.

"You'd still be with Mom." Gunner regretted the words as soon as they came out of his mouth. "Sorry, Dad, I didn't mean to..."

Silas smiled a sad smile and shook his head cutting off Gunner's words. "I loved her with everything I had. She just couldn't fight her demons any longer." He swallowed hard and then shook his head. "We had a good life, right up until the day she quit fighting. I won't tarnish what we had by remembering how it ended. She was the love of my life."

Gunner stepped across the three feet that separated him from his father and pulled him into a hug. "I love you, Dad. You've always been there for me. You've always been my hero. Never doubt that. I'm so lucky to be your son."

"Love you, too, kiddo." His dad nodded and squeezed him tighter for just a moment before letting go and stepping back. "Now, go take a shower, because I'm not going to tell you what you smell like." Silas glanced over toward A.J.'s house. "I'll give her a half hour or so before I go knock on the door and remind her *we* have a date. See you tonight."

Gunner watched his father walk away. The old man made it to the pub every night and usually had the company of a silver-haired beauty. His mother had been gone a long time and Gunner was happy to see his father with an active social life. He tossed his keys in the bowl by the door, locked the front door behind him and headed to the shower. He was looking forward to work tonight and what would come after. Saturday nights were always busy. It was a good thing the pub was closed on Sundays because Gunner had every intention of keeping A.J. awake until the sun came up.

~

A.J. glanced over the bar and caught Silas's eye. She motioned with her head silently asking him to meet her at the end of the bar. He excused himself from his conversation and made his way to her.

"What's up?" He leaned on his forearms.

"I need to ask you a question. I should have thought to do it when we were walking today, but my mind was elsewhere."

"I know where your mind was, young lady." Silas's gruff words struck her. She gazed up at him. His face contorted and then he laughed merrily. "Hey, when your dad asks, tell him I tried, okay?"

"You are an instigator, Silas Kincade!" A.J. flicked him with the bar towel she had in her hand. "My father loves the fact that you've taken me under your wing. Now let me ask you my question while the customers are satisfied."

"Okay, hit me with it." Silas reached for the party mix container on the employee's side of the bar and poured himself a dishful.

"What's Gunner's favorite meal? I told him I'd cook him dinner tomorrow night."

"Easy. Linguini and mussels. Throw in a loaf of crusty bread, and a salad and that boy would eat himself into a comma. Better double whatever recipe you use. He'll eat you out of house and home." Silas took his bowl of bar mix and winked at her. "It runs in the family."

A.J. watched him go back to his booth and glanced down the bar. Gunner had just refilled a Manhattan and was making a martini. In another month or so, the man would be able to handle the bar by himself even at peak capacity.

She was not really pondering his competency as a bartender. She was seriously considering whether or not to attempt to make a meal she had no idea how to cook. *Mussels and linguini. Damn. Really?* Being from East Texas, her mother taught her how to cook a host of things, beef, pork, chicken, lamb, buffalo, venison, antelope, rabbit, quail, pheasant...but never mussels. She could bake the bread and make the noodles for the dish from scratch but had no idea how to cook mussels. A quick internet search for linguini and mussels was in order. She made sure Gunner was good to go and then entered linguini and mussels into the search bar of her web browser. The first recipe she saw was from a renowned television chef. The first ingredient was two pounds of live, debearded mussels. *Mussels have beards?* A.J.'s head popped up. *Did they come debearded or would she have to...shave them?* She glanced at Gunner who was busy pouring another draft. *Why couldn't you like prime rib or leg of lamb or even roasted turkey? Those* things she could knock out of the park.

"Dear, may I have another Chardonnay?"

A.J. jumped and pocketed her phone. "Of course,

I'm sorry, Ms. Wade." She reached for the open bottle of Chardonnay at her end of the bar and poured the sweet lady a new glass.

"You were deep in thought; I stood there for a while before I spoke. What were you concentrating so hard on, if you don't mind me asking?" Charlotte Wade took a seat at the bar. It was still early, and most of her senior customers would be leaving soon when the younger and rowdier crowd took over the space.

"I was researching how to make linguini and mussels. Did you know mussels had beards?" A.J. set the glass of wine on the bar and accepted the twenty-dollar bill, turning her back to make change.

She glanced up at the mirror and saw a smile spread across Charlotte's face. "Yes, dear, I did."

A.J. got her change and spun around. "Excellent! Do they come debearded or will I have to do that?"

"Oh, most of the mussels sold around here around here are farm raised. They will be debearded, but you need to check each one just in case. The beards are inedible. They are these little things on the outside edge of the mussel's shell. Grab it with a paper towel and yank it toward the hinge of the clam, not straight out. It comes out easy enough, but you have to give it a firm yank."

"Awesome. Thank you so much. You are a lifesaver." A.J. leaned in to ask more questions, but a large party poured through the front door. Gunner glanced her way, and she smiled. It was time for the busy part of the night to commence. She glanced at Charlotte. "Thanks again."

"No problem, dear. If you need help, Silas knows my number." Charlotte slid off the stool and headed toward the back of the pub where Silas was holding court. A.J. saw the look that passed between the two of them as Charlotte approached. She had no doubt Silas had the woman's number. No doubt whatsoever.

CHAPTER 10

A.J. counted out the cash and ran the receipts against the total the register had spit out the second the doors were locked. It was her second and last time through the numbers. Thankfully they matched so she didn't have to go looking for an unclosed tab or accounting error. There was a sense of urgency tonight. At least for her, although she assumed it was the same for the man across the room. Gunner had practically run through breaking down the bar and cleaning tonight. Her gaze lingered on him, surprised at the turn of events during the last twenty-four hours.

She lowered her eyes and concentrated on completing the bank deposit for the night instead of letting her thoughts linger on her new lover. Tender touches and whispered endearments notwithstanding, they'd managed to behave professionally behind the bar tonight. Which was harder than she'd actually thought it would be. Keeping her attention focused on the customers rather than the six-feet-four-inch man currently mopping the floor was difficult. Especially when his muscles played under the tightly stretched black cotton bearing the Wayward Walrus' logo. Tonight, black jeans encased those thick, delicious thighs. A.J.'s eyes drifted to the dark wood under the unfinished deposit slip. She shivered at the memory of wrapping her legs around him as he made love to her.

Not that he was actually making love to her. They were...well, they were having sex. She knew insta-love only happened on those television channels created for women. The perfect lover, perfect timing, instant attraction and a happily ever after. Her relationship thus far with Gunner was anything but perfect. Her face heated. Except when they were in bed, because that, well, that was perfect. Absolutely perfect. She glanced over at Gunner and smiled. The man was so unlike Marcus, and for that, she was thankful. Taking Gunner to her bed last night had been a leap of faith.

She hadn't been with anyone since Marcus. When the person who claimed to love you almost kills you, it has an effect. Oh, she tried to be brave, to stand her ground, but when push came to shove, she'd left. It was easy to convince herself she was protecting her family, but with miles between her and the insinuations and intimidation of Marcus's brothers, she could admit she was really protecting herself. In that tiny one-horse town everyone knew her business. They knew the intimate details of her and Marcus's relationship. It had all come out at the trial. Marcus's lawyer had tried to paint her as a horrid woman, he'd tried to get the jury to see her as evil and manipulative and that her cheating was the reason Marcus had lost his temper. She'd never cheated. Never. Ultimately, the smear tactics hadn't worked, but people talked. They whispered behind her back or just glared at her, depending on who she was facing. Marcus's family may have come from the wrong side of the tracks, but they had friends.

The fact that his brothers had repeatedly threatened her, ignoring the restraining order that was in place, was the excuse she needed. She ran and kept running until she felt safe. She found that sense of security and belonging here at Half Moon Bay. So much so that she'd used her share of the inheritance her grandfather had left to her and her siblings to buy into the Walrus.

Getting close to Gunner was a risk, but one she was finally willing to take. A smooth whistled tune graced the quietness of the empty bar. The sound was eerily beautiful. She glanced up and smiled as he tossed a look her way. A sense of peaceful contentment fell in place around her. A sensation completely foreign to her yet utterly perfect. Yes, she was ready to take a chance on love again.

"Are you almost ready to go?" Gunner's voice startled her.

"In just a minute." It took less to fill out the bank slip. She shoved the money and slip into the cash pouch. "Ready."

Gunner placed his hand on the small of her back and escorted her out of the bar. The warmth of his touch stayed with her during her drive to the bank and home. She pulled into her garage and glanced up at the rearview mirror, waiting. As soon as he slipped into the garage she hit the button secluding them from the world.

He opened her car door and held his hand out to her.

"Such a gentleman." She let him assist her from the car and shut the door after she exited.

Gunner lifted her hand to his lips and kissed the back, while watching her. "I can be when the situation calls for it."

A.J.'s breath caught in her throat. She had proof he could be tender and caring, but... "And when the situation requires a rogue?"

"A rogue?" His arm snapped out and seized her against him. "Be sure you know what you're asking for."

A.J. felt the blood pounding in her veins. She wanted to see and feel this man, uninhibited and unrestrained. "Dear sir, would you be so kind as to ravish me?"

The growl deep in his throat was the only warning she got. A.J. squealed as he dipped and threw her over his shoulder. As soon as she realized what he was doing she laughed and held on. It took less than a minute to be flopped onto her bed. He stripped in less than thirty seconds and then her clothes were gone without any fanfare. Gunner dropped an accordion strip of condoms onto the bed and pounced. A.J. shrieked, laughing at the way his beard tickled her neck. His fingers played over her ribs and under her arms. She laughed until she cried, "Uncle! I give!"

Gunner lifted over her on his hands and knees. "Ravishing over already, my lady?"

She held her hand against his chest just in case he decided to start tickling her again. "I'm not quite sure that was what I meant."

He dropped a kiss to her shoulder. "I know." A trail of kisses across her collar bone ended on the other shoulder. "I'm sure there will be times that desperation forces us to go faster, but not tonight. Tonight, I want to learn every inch of your body. I want to find the places that drive you insane."

His fingers trailed lightly over one breast causing her to shiver. He blew on her nipple; the sensuous effect elicited a gasp. She closed her eyes and ran her fingers over his skin as he set about lighting a fire deep within her core. She traced a scar on his shoulder before she levered herself up far enough to kiss it. He lifted his eyes from where he was mapping her body. The heat in his gaze sent shivers of desire across her skin.

"You are beautiful," he whispered against her skin.

A.J. closed her eyes and lost herself in the revelation of this man—his touches and her body's responses.

She ran her fingers through his hair. "I want to touch you, too."

He hummed as he parted her legs and nestled between them. "Later. My turn." A.J. grasped ahold of his hair and moaned. The sensation of his mouth on her...she'd never experienced such complete concentration on her needs and for the first time in her life, she let go and dropped her guard. Never had a man treated her with such tenderness, respect and...oh, yes...pure unadulterated want.

His return up the skin of her torso to her lips was just as sensuous, but her body needed him inside her. "Please. Gunner. Please." She panted the pleas.

"Now, baby?" He lowered his lips to hers and consumed her with a kiss that left her out of her mind with need.

"Now." She gasped the word when he released her from the devastating connection.

He lifted away, ripped open a condom package and rolled it onto his cock all the while staring at her like she was the center of his universe. A.J.'s sex-addled brain realized that look, that need, was something she'd never seen before, and it was something she realized she never wanted to live without.

He wrapped her in his arms and entered her with slow, grinding thrust. A.J. wrapped her legs around him and feasted on the expanse of skin over her. The restrained power above her was palpable. Her hands mapped his chest and his arms as his rhythm increased and the force of his body pushed her closer to her release. He moved her leg, lifting it up to his hip.

She gasped at the impact the slight change brought. "Yes!"

He smiled and lowered for a kiss. "Ready to be ravished, my lady?"

She moaned at the sensations floating inside her, just under the skin, ready to erupt. "Oh, god, yes."

He snapped his hips. The angle and force joined perfectly to push her over the edge. She heard the echo of her scream as her body drew into an immense contraction of sensation and then exploded into the atmosphere.

A.J. struggled to breathe as she gathered herself from the detonation. She felt him tense and heard his shout as he released. His face was a study of masculine splendor. He dropped his head onto her shoulder.

She ran her hands through his sweat soaked hair and found the breath to chuckle. He lifted his head and arched an eyebrow at her. "Not what a man wants to hear after some of the best sex of his life."

She let out another breathless chuckle, "No, I was thinking if this was what it was like when we weren't desperate, I don't know if I'll survive when we finally get to that point."

He dropped for a quick kiss. "Don't worry, my lady. Survival is guaranteed."

Gunner emerged from the bay after his morning swim. He'd been promptly kicked out of A.J.'s house this morning after a night of spectacular sex. The woman was a tornado of action even first thing in the morning. He dropped to the sand in a harder packed area of the beach and got into position to do pushups, all while thinking about this morning's conversation.

"I have to go shopping. I have this apology dinner to make for this guy that I kicked in the balls." She blinked innocently at him.

He grunted and pulled her closer. The feel of her soft skin against his was addictive, and he did not want to get up yet. "I don't think the guy needs an apology dinner anymore."

"Oh no. Groveling was required. Groveling shall commence." She hopped out of bed and extended her hand to him. *"But I think I do have time for a shower."*

That little bit of fire and sass was quickly on her way to becoming very important to him. Gunner chuckled as he started his count. The feel of his muscles working, the strain of his core, back, and shoulders as he exercised was exactly what he needed. Exercise always cleared his head so he could think clearer.

"Son, I've never been able to do that many pushups."

Gunner lifted his head for a moment before dropping it again, keeping his pace. "Practice. Pops." He grunted each word, one on the decline and one on the pushup. He'd lost count, but the burn of his muscles told him he needed to press on. He wasn't near his limit yet.

His father's walking shoes came into view. He could tell his dad was facing the bay, but he spoke loud enough to be heard over the breeze that always blew in from the ocean. "Charlotte and I are going to head into San Francisco for the day. May not be back tonight. There is a Broadway play that is on tour. She's mentioned wanting to see it a couple times. Thought I might take her. Spend the night, so we don't have to drive back that late."

Gunner stopped in the up position and dropped to his knees. Sitting back on his heels he smiled up at his dad. "Good on you, old man."

His father put his hands in his pockets and kept staring out at the bay. "I loved your momma with all my heart. This doesn't take anything away from that."

Gunner lifted to his feet and grabbed his swim fins. He turned and watched the water with his father for a moment before he spoke, taking the time to arrange his thoughts so his words sent the right message to his dad. "Mom has been gone for a hell of a long time now, Pops. You've grieved. You've built a life beyond what we once had. It is alright to push forward, to find happiness. If Charlotte is that happiness, I'm fucking thrilled for you. You can't diminish what was with what is happening now. Two different phases of the same life." He turned to his dad. "If you are asking for my permission, I'll give it to you."

His father slowly shook his head, still staring out toward the water. "No, I wasn't asking for permission. Just informing you of my intentions. I realized a long time ago I needed to move on, but nobody has ever made me want to go that direction, until Charlotte. She's an amazing woman. Has three grown children of her own. Her husband died ten years back. Cancer."

"I hope you have a wonderful time, Dad. Enjoy the show and enjoy your time with Charlotte. If you want, take a couple days. A.J. and I can handle the Walrus. We should be back up to full staff." Hell, they'd manage even if someone called out sick. He and A.J. made a pretty damn good team behind the bar.

"No, one night is a big enough adventure for us. I'm heading out to pick her up in about a half hour. Just wanted to let you know." Silas turned and started up the grass-covered lawn. Gunner fell in next to him picking his way through the sharpest rocks. He really needed to dig out his water shoes. They were buried somewhere in the box of exercise equipment he had in the garage. "How are things with A.J.?"

Gunner darted a quick look at his dad. There was no indication of teasing, so he went with an honest answer. "Surprisingly well. She hasn't injured or attempted to kill me in the past twenty-four hours, so I call that a win."

His father stopped and glanced at his watch. "That means the day before yesterday she did attempt to maim or kill you?" A mischievous expression slid across his father's face.

Gunner gave a small chuckle and rubbed the back of his neck. "Well, there was an incident. Kind of a meeting of two minds via a skull cracking type incident. Knocked both of us on our butts. That woman has a hard head."

His dad shook his head and laughed, stepping once again towards his house. "In more ways than one. If I leave you two alone tonight, promise me you won't end up the hospital?"

"I can't promise you that. The woman is a minefield. One wrong step and...boom!" His hands flew up into the air as he said the last word.

His father laughed and slapped him on the back. "Well, enjoy the adventure, kiddo."

"I will. You enjoy your evening and tell Charlotte I said hello."

"Will do." His father smiled, winked and headed took the path to his house. Gunner broke off to walk the other path to his home. A huge sigh of contentment filled his lungs. He was happy and fuck it if it wasn't an amazing feeling. Any notion that his retirement wasn't the right decision had long since departed. Life at this moment was fucking spectacular.

CHAPTER 11

The house smelled fantastic. The baguettes A.J. had just pulled out of the oven were perfectly golden brown. Her homemade linguini noodles were lightly dusted with flour to keep them from sticking together before she dropped them into boiling, salted water. The last thing she needed to do for prep was to wash and debeard the mussels. Pulling up the recipe again she read it through. Simple enough. Using a small brush she'd bought on her shopping trip this morning, she scrubbed the outside of the mussels as she took the little shells out of the bag. There were one or two that had the little beards on the shells and a couple of the shells that were open. Holding the shell at eye level, she looked inside. The snot-like thing inside the dark brown shell solidified the fact she was eating a salad and bread for dinner. She cringed and shivered at the idea of putting hard shells into a bowl of noodles, let alone serving them, but if Gunner liked this dish, she'd follow the directions to a "T." She clicked the open mussel in her hand like a castanet and laughed at her silliness. It would be easier if all the shells were open. Then she could scoop the snotty little critters out and not have to put the shells in the pasta. But only five or six of the shells were open, and she had no idea how to make the rest open up without cooking them. Whatever. She put all the mussels into a strainer and was finally to a point where she could go get herself ready for the evening.

A.J. took her time in the shower and afterward putting on makeup and fixing her hair. Both were things she rarely bothered doing. Typically, she washed her face, scraped her hair back in a ponytail and went to work. Tonight, however, she wanted to take the time to look nice for Gunner. Was it silly and perhaps a little bit vain? Maybe, but the butterflies in her stomach told her it was important. She opened her dresser and pulled out a small box. She removed the top and gently lifted the thin, fancy paper that covered the contents, a lace thong with matching bra and wrap that cost far too much money. A.J. snorted at the price she paid. Probably close to ten dollars per square inch of lace. But they were beautiful, and she couldn't wait to see Gunner's face when she put them on for him tonight. She carefully hung up the lace and placed them on the back of the bathroom door. She put a pair of white stilettos along the sink vanity out of view. If all went according to plan, she'd excuse herself, change and then make a grand entrance.

Her face heated at the thought. She wasn't a seductress. She was a small-town girl from East Texas, but she'd concluded she wanted Gunner for more than just a fling. She felt sexy, safe and cherished in his arms, and she wanted that feeling to grow and flourish. The pretty little bits of lace weren't necessary, but she wanted to try.

Her face and hair done and wearing a little black wrap-around dress she'd bought for a wedding years ago, A.J. slipped on her heels and headed back to the kitchen. She pulled the salad out of the refrigerator and pulled the cork on the bottle of Merlot she'd purchased earlier. She placed an aerator on the top of the bottle and poured herself a small glass to have along with a rather large piece of fresh bread she unabashedly slathered with butter. She pulled up the recipe again, reached into the fridge to pull out the ingredients she'd prepped earlier, and turned on the burner to bring the water to boil. According to the recipe, it would take only minutes to cook the mussels. She wanted the water for the pasta hot and ready to go. Putting a lid on the pot, she finished her bread and drank the last of her wine.

A second glass of wine poured, she wandered out to the back porch of her little rental house. It was smaller than Silas's home. The house Gunner lived in had been a rental at one time, but she could tell that he'd modified the house over the years. She sat down in one of the two chairs she had on the porch and watched the water. A flicker of movement caught her eye. Gunner walked out of his house wearing a long sleeve white shirt, grey dress slacks, and carried a bouquet of roses. Her heart fluttered in her chest. She'd never received flowers, let alone roses, from a boyfriend. Her mind stumbled over that adjective, but somehow, she let herself believe Gunner was her boyfriend, not just a hook-up.

He jogged up her back steps and leaned over, dropping a kiss on her upturned lips as he lay the flowers in her arms. She pulled them up and buried her nose into the soft pedals before she smiled up at him. "Thank you, but I thought I was supposed to be groveling tonight."

He sat down beside her and stretched out his long legs. "I told you groveling was not necessary. I'll even take you out to dinner to prove it."

"Oh, no." They were eating a meal she prepared especially for him, and she had a fashion show, of sorts, planned for dessert. "No, I have everything ready. I just need to drop the pasta—which is home-made, by the way, because I wanted you to know when I grovel, I grovel professionally. First, would you like a glass of wine?"

Gunner looked at the glass and chuckled. "I can do wine with dinner, but I'm a single malt type of guy."

"Ah, well then I have a small amount of Lagavulin or a full bottle of Macallan. Do you prefer it over ice?" She lifted out of the chair as she spoke. He made a move to get up, and she held up her hand stopping him. "I need to put these in water. We can watch the sunset." She nodded toward the bay. For once it was clear and relatively warm. She would grab a shawl on the way out.

"In that case, I'd like to try the Macallan. Are you sure I can't help?" He moved to get out of the chair again.

She touched his shoulder, freezing his motion. "Let me do this. It's included in the price of groveling." She held her roses to her nose again and smiled into the flowers as she turned and practically danced into the kitchen.

It took a few minutes to find a vase, but she succeeded and placed the flowers on the sofa table where they dominated the small living room-slash-dining room combination. His single malt poured, she grabbed a crocheted shawl and headed out to the small porch. After handing him his scotch, she settled into her chair and turned to him. "Tell me about being a Navy SEAL."

He gave her a surprised glance before he looked back out to the bay. She wasn't sure if he was uncomfortable with the question or not sure how to answer her. Just as she was about to laugh it off and ask a different question, he spoke.

"It was all I ever wanted to do. Growing up I found an article in some obscure magazine at school. I think I was a freshman in high school at the time, maybe a sophomore, I don't really remember. What I do remember is reading about the physical and mental demands placed on the candidates. They had these pictures throughout the article. The men were filthy, and you could see the exhaustion on their faces, but there was this one guy. He wasn't the focus of the photograph. He stood behind the man the photo was about. He had this look of complete determination in his eyes. Everyone else had looks of anguish, but this guy, it was like he'd channeled this inner Zen or something. You didn't see the strain like you could on the guys surrounding him. That guy fascinated me. Later in the article, it showed the graduating class. The article said the attrition rate was seventy-five to eighty percent. Only twenty to twenty-five men out of a hundred were able to make it through the training. The man I picked out in the other picture, he graduated. Again, he wasn't the focus of the picture, but he was there and still with that look of complete and utter calm on his face. I knew then that I wanted to be that guy."

A.J. was enthralled. Gunner's expression was so intense, yet calm. It was almost like he'd channeled the picture he'd talked about. "So, you joined the Navy after high school or college?"

"I enlisted after high school." He chuckled and shook his head. "I thought I had a clue on how tough going through BUD/S would be, but shit, there is no way to prepare for that. No way in hell."

"Buds? What is that?"

"B.U.D. slash S. It stands for Basic Underwater Demolition slash SEAL training." He shrugged. "Until you are pushed to your limits you don't know really what your limits are and what you are willing to endure to reach your goal. The course is made to tear you down. To get those who aren't strong enough, physically and mentally, to drop. Sometimes physical injuries cause a person to drop, but most of the time the course defeats your mind before it defeats your body. Hell, I can remember it like I lived it yesterday. I was ready to quit. We were freezing cold and ten hours into the worst twenty-four hours of my fucking life, but right before I opened my mouth to tap out, that guy's face flashed through my mind. I latched onto that ideal. I'd played with the whole Zen thing through high school. It earned me my nick-name." He chuckled and rubbed his beard. "They called me Iceman. I fucking ate that shit up. Big man on campus, you know. Quarterback. Well, that didn't mean shit when I was blue with cold and wanting nothing more than to quit. Right then, I finally got what that man was doing. He'd found a place inside of himself stronger than the elements that surrounded him. I turned inward, and I searched until I found that place." He shrugged. "I made it through the remaining fourteen hours and graduated before I went on to other schools and training."

A.J. took a sip of her wine and waited for him to sip his scotch. "Are the movies true? Is that what SEALs really do?"

"Movies? Hell, I never watched any of those. I have no idea what they depict. I trained hard, every day. I was part of a team, and we did routine deployments. Those that weren't necessarily routine were few and far between, but that is why we train. We do what the nation asks us to do. We do it to the best of our ability. Somehow the media caught wind of a couple of the missions one team was involved in, and suddenly a profession that lived below the radar was exposed, glorified and vilified, all at the same time." He turned and met her stare with his. "I served my country. It is as simple as that. Every person on my team would lay down his life for me as I would lay down my life for them." A smirk spread across his face, "But I can guarantee you, should some force try to take us out, hell on earth would erupt before we went down. We are that good." He blinked and then took a sip of his whiskey. "Was that good. I'm out of it now."

A.J. ran her finger across the lip of her wine glass as the sun started to fall behind the horizon. "Do you regret getting out? Silas said once he didn't want you to get out because of his stroke. He didn't want you to make that sacrifice."

She watched as his gaze floated back to the water. "I miss the men on my team. Hell, they were my family for twenty years. Of course people transitioned, left for one reason or another, but you go through some of the things we went through together, and you get tight. I won't deny I miss that, but it was time. Young men come in and take our places. It is the way of all services. When Dad had his stroke, I was at a point in my career where I was questioning when to punch my ticket. I'm good with my decision." He glanced at her. "What about you? Are you happy with your decision to move to Half Moon Bay?"

A.J. considered his question for a moment. "I'm not thrilled with the reason I left home. I wish my lessons in trusting and loving the wrong person hadn't resulted in a week-long stay in the hospital and then a month's recuperation." His hand landed on hers, and she linked fingers with him. He squeezed her hand, and a soft smile spread as warmth filled his eyes. "I adored your father from the moment I met him. He is a class act. I could tell he had physical limitations. He didn't use his arm, and his speech was slightly slurred, but his wit was sharp, and he made me laugh. I worked hard during that interview. For some reason I needed him to know he could count on me to run the Walrus and to run it correctly."

"He's very impressed with you." Gunner lifted their joined hand and kissed her knuckles. "So am I."

Her heart fluttered, and her insides flipped just a little. She didn't know how to respond. Flustered, she stood, pulling their hands apart. "I'm...I'm going to go start dinner. Can I get you another drink?"

He chuckled and shook his head, lifting his nearly

untouched glass of Macallan. "I'm good. Do you need any help?"

She shook her head and laughed. "No. Required groveling, remember? Finish your drink before you come in. Dinner will be ready in no time."

A.J. drew a deep breath the second the door to the porch closed. She put her hands to her face and smiled. She felt like a teenage girl with her first crush. Was she happy with her move to Half Moon Bay? No, she was ecstatic!

CHAPTER 12

*G*unner gazed over the water. The sounds from inside the kitchen played like distant background music to his musings. Memories of a childhood spent on his father's back porch hastened to mind. His mother's laugh as his pops picked her up and spun her. The nights he and his old man had lain under the stars and talked about everything and nothing. Life here was everything he ever wanted for his family, should he ever be so lucky. At forty it wasn't guaranteed. He lingered outside in the growing darkness until the irresistible smell of garlic sent his stomach into a roar that would do a pride of lions proud. He finished the last of his whiskey and wandered in the house.

Two long tapered candles were lit on a small table immaculately set for two. A single red rose was placed in a tall glass in the middle of the candles. With the exception of the kitchen, none of the house lights were on. The small area off the kitchen had been set as a scene of seduction that even he, a salty old SEAL, could understand. He leaned against the kitchen counter and watched as she strained a pot of noodles. To his wonder and amazement, she lifted the lid to a wonderful sight. He lifted away from the counter and stepped behind her, putting his hand on her back in an effort to stop her from startling. It worked. She smiled up at him. "Your dad said linguini and mussels were your favorite."

"I haven't had them in a long time." His tastes had changed over the years, but his dad was right, linguini and mussels were still one of his favorites. "This smells wonderful."

"Thank you. I'll have you know, for you, I learned how to tear the beard off mussels. I wasn't aware groveling required learning how to shave shellfish, but shave them I did."

Gunner looked at her and then back at the mussels. "You didn't actually shave them, did you?"

A.J. laughed and filled a large bowl with noodles. The salads and bread were already on the table. "No, Charlotte explained how to debeard them."

"Well I, for one, cannot wait to eat the feast before me." "I'm glad because I have to admit, I'm not eating those." A.J. poked the opened shells with a serving spoon. She lifted a few up. They dripped what smelled like white wine sauce. "They look like..." she glanced up at him and whispered, "... snot and who puts shells in pasta?"

He blinked at her and then looked at the mussels before he started laughing. She was fucking adorable. "You made me a dinner you have no intentions of eating?"

She squinted at him and then at the pot where she poked at the top shell again. "Well, yeah. Your dad said it was your favorite."

"So is a thick juicy ribeye or any type of pulled pork." He grabbed a shell out of the pot and jostled it in his fingers before he tipped his head back and popped the mussel into his mouth. The flavor of garlic, butter and white wine exploded on his tongue. The sauce was going to be amazing over her home-cooked noodles. He rolled his eyes heavenward before he leaned down and kissed her hard on the lips. "Perfection."

She lit up from the inside. "Really? As you can guess from the shaving comment, I've never cooked this before. I hope it's good." She ladled several large spoonfuls of seafood and sauce over the noodles and handed him the bowl. "Take that to the table. Would you like another scotch, or do you want wine with dinner?"

"Scotch, please. The Macallan was very good." Gunner placed the bowl at his seat and only then noticed the larger salad centered at her place setting. She wasn't joking, she'd spent all day making a dinner she wasn't going to eat. He waited until she returned with his drink and a full glass of wine for herself. He pulled her chair out for her and seated her, bending over to kiss her lightly on the lips. "Thank you for the effort you put into dinner."

She blushed prettily and smiled at him. "You're most welcome."

Gunner sat down and stared at the bowl in front of him. He couldn't help thinking that her efforts were more than just groveling. Or at least he'd hope there was more behind the homemade noodles, fresh bread and the hassle of making a dish she'd never made before.

"Please, dig in. I'm dying to know if you like the noodles. My grandmother taught my sisters and me how to make them. The woman literally never used a packaged noodle in her life." A.J. speared some fancy looking lettuce and lifted it to her mouth as Gunner dug in. The noodles were complete heaven. The white wine sauce had a hint of citrus and a wallop of garlic.

"Amazing. Perfect. And the noodles. Seriously, can I pay you to make me spaghetti sometime"? It was fucking fantastic.

She laughed and shook her head. "No. I'll make it for free. No payment necessary. We can invite Silas and Charlotte over."

"Hell of an idea." He took another bite and grabbed the hunk of fresh bread from his plate. "Excuse me, but my table manners have gone to shit." He dipped the bread into the sauce and moaned at the taste combination.

"I grew up in a house where fingers were considered utensils. Eat and enjoy."

Gunner did. He ate until he was uncomfortably full. It wasn't his intention when he came over here. Getting A.J. into bed had been the game plan, but the conversation and food were damn good.

A.J. was funny and engaging to the point he looked up and noticed they'd been talking for thirty minutes over the empty plates. Her east Texas upbringing took his rough-around-the-edges self and made him feel comfortable, wanted and accepted. He leaned away from the empty shells in his bowl and lifted his Macallan in her direction. "A toast to the chef. That was an amazing meal."

"Thank you." She took a sip of her wine and looked at him under her lashes as she lowered her glass. "I do have dessert."

The look she gave him sent a delicious twitch to his cock. "I love desserts of all varieties, but..." He dropped his hand to his flat but hella-full stomach. "I need a couple minutes. How about we adjourn to the porch and listen to the water and visit for a while before we serve up dessert."

With another one of those cock-stirring smiles, she nodded. He stood and held out his hand to her. She rose, and he took the opportunity to fold her into his arms, kissing her the way he'd wanted to kiss her when he'd arrived tonight. Her warm, sensual body fit perfectly against him, and fuck, the woman tasted like red wine and sin. Hell, he would definitely order her for dessert. He broke the kiss and held her against him.

"This is nice." Her words were muffled, but he couldn't agree more. "I should take care of the dishes."

"Let's just stack them in the sink, and we can worry about them in the morning." He let her pull away so he could see her face. The small amount of makeup she'd used made the green of her eyes more intense. She didn't need makeup, and he'd never seen her wear it before, so it had to be an effort made for him. He lowered and kissed her nose. "Did I tell you how beautiful you look tonight?"

"No." She shook her head and continued to stare at him.

"Well then, I'm a moron. You, Miss Amanda Jean, look exceedingly beautiful tonight." He watched her smile at his words.

"I never liked that name." She stepped back breaking their embrace. She walked backward toward the sink, and he followed. Neither of them had dishes in their hands.

"Why not. Amanda is a beautiful name." He pinned her against the counter, one arm on either side of her as he leaned down with his legs extended behind him, so he was more on her level.

"Because my name isn't Amanda, it is Amanda Jean. Kind of like Billy Bob. You know us Texas people with two name first names." There was a definite flush to her face.

"There is a simple solution for that. You're in California now. Drop the Jean. You can be Amanda Ericson. Nobody has to know." He dropped his lips to hers. "Amanda."

"Isn't that like telling a lie?" She whispered when he pulled away.

He shook his head and lowered for another kiss. He stopped a millimeter from her lips. "No, it isn't." He took her mouth with a little more force. The woman could kiss. Their tongues dueled until he needed to surface for air. By her gasp, A.J. was nearly as breathless.

"I need to..." She grabbed both of his arms and took another breath "I mean...I need to stop...I need to do the dishes."

Well, that was not what he expected. Surprised, he started to step away, but she held onto his arm. "I need to do the dishes before I climb that big, tall, hard body of yours and attack you like a sex-crazed maniac."

He felt his smile spread across his face. *Well all right then, that was better.* "I'll help, and then we can revisit the climbing topic."

"Lord have mercy." She mumbled the words under her breath as she slipped under his arm and headed to the small dining room table.

Gunner blew out the candles as the last of the dishes were taken to the kitchen. They worked together to put the rinsed plates, bowls and utensils in the small dishwasher. Gunner refilled their drinks, and they floated out onto the porch. As much as he'd like to take her directly to bed, his meal wasn't settling as fast as he'd like. As a matter of fact, he must have eaten more than he realized. His stomach was not particularly happy with him right now. But, he had an iron gut. Too many deployments eating MREs had put an iron lining around his stomach. All he needed was a few minutes to let dinner settle and dessert could be served. He was really looking forward to what she had on the menu. The woman was turning into a never-ending surprise.

He extended a hand and A.J. joined him in his chair, snuggling onto his lap. He propped his chin on the top of her head and stared out into the darkness. The sounds of the waves lapping the water made for a soothing background. They sat like that for several long minutes. Comfortable and content.

"Have I told you that I like the way you hold me?" Her fingers ran up and down his forearm.

He moved her a little, giving his stomach some space while he simultaneously tightened his grip, pulling her into his chest. "No. Have I told you that I like holding you?"

She giggled. A real no-shit giggle. The innocence in that sound made his heart puff up and pound just a little harder.

"I like whatever this is, Gunner. I hope you do, too."

"I do." His stomach rolled, and he swallowed hard. A wave of nausea careened through his gut, and it wasn't silent.

A.J. sat up, spinning to look at him. Gunner felt a wave of heat blast through him, then he started to swallow hard. He shook his head. *Fuck, no, no, no!* Launching out of the chair he upended A.J. and sending her stumbling toward the rail. He flew into the house and slammed the bathroom door behind him. It took less than ten seconds of projectile vomiting to render him a heap beside the toilet. The next three minutes lasted an eternity. Gunner fought back a tsunami of nausea to no avail. He grabbed the porcelain and let his body violently expel what felt like his stomach lining. And then...fuck, he tightly clenched his muscles praying as he fumbled with his slacks. Freeing the button and slamming the zipper down at the last second, he fell onto the toilet. He groaned as his stomach twisted tight, cramped, and...oh, *God...please just kill me now.*

CHAPTER 13

*D*isbelief drenched her as she stood on the other side of the door. She turned and looked at the kitchen and grimaced at the sound of Gunner as he was sick. *Oh shit. Shit, shit, shit, shit!* She ran to the kitchen and grabbed her cell phone off the counter and opened the browser immediately and typed: *Can mussels give you food poisoning?*

Her hand flew to her mouth as she read the words of the first article. *Oh my God! The opened mussels! They were bad.* How was she supposed to know? The recipe didn't say anything about opened shells. Nothing. A low, miserable sounding moan originating from behind the bathroom door jolted her into action. She flew to the door and lifted her hand to knock. Another agonizing moan and then...oh no.

The clenched fist perched precariously close to knocking dropped, and she stepped away from the door. *How would you feel if someone knocked when you were...?* A low, deep, pathetic sound reached her ears before she heard him retch again.

He needs his privacy.

But you need to make sure he's okay. You did this to him.

Again.

She hated herself more in that moment than she could have ever imagined. The toilet flushed again. What could she do? Gripping her phone so it didn't shake in her hand, she typed into the browser: *What do for food poisoning.*

A.J.'s back hit the wall of the small hall outside the bathroom door, and she slid down, landing in a very inelegant heap. She scrolled through the medical pages. She suffered outside the door as he suffered inside. Why did this need to happen? What had she done to jinx this relationship? Had the stars and Mercury aligned, so the world crapped on anything that happened between the two of them? She wiped a tear away from her cheek. He'd been silent for a long time. She crawled to the door and sat down outside it before she knocked quietly. There was no response. "I'm so sorry."

That got her a grunt. It was something.

She lifted the phone as if he could see it and told him, "I think maybe some of the mussels were bad."

"Really? You think?" Gunner's low, hoarse voice drifted from the other side of the door.

A.J. flinched. Gunner sounded as if he sat on the floor just opposite her. She dropped her head back against the wall, and the tears of frustration fell. "I'm always apologizing to you for messing up. I didn't know the open mussels were bad. I'm so sorry." He had to believe her. She closed her eyes tightly, but more tears oozed out to trickle down her cheeks. "What can I do?"

"Just..." A retching sound followed. She closed her eyes as he dealt with the results of her meal. It was several minutes before he spoke again.

"Please, could you just leave. I know this is your house. Stay at mine, but, please...just...oh, God..." His misery seemed to be the ongoing theme of their relationship.

A.J. wiped her tears and stood up. She could give him that, at least—a shred of dignity in a degrading and humiliating situation. One she took ownership of. She packed a small bag in less than five minutes and left a note taped to the door jamb of the bathroom telling him she'd gone to a hotel. The door jamb was the only place she could guarantee he'd see the note.

He'd passed out on bathroom floors before. He wasn't proud of that fact. Too young and too much alcohol was the basis for a lot of shitty decisions. However, he had no words for this morning's agony. Rolling onto his back, he slowly opened his eyes and blinked repeatedly. He hadn't even turned off the light when physical exhaustion knocked his ass out. He lifted an arm and shaded his eyes. Fuck, his head felt like he'd drank a full bottle of Scotch by himself. He blinked up at the ceiling and as his gaze slowly lowered, his eyes rested on the bathroom door. It took him several seconds to piece together what he saw hanging on the back of the door. A white lace bra and panties hung on one hanger a lace cover-up on another. *Fuck him.* He could imagine A. J. in those pieces of lace until the morbid embarrassment of exactly what happened last night played out in his mind. *Yeah, fuck him twice.*

He swallowed and cringed at the taste in his mouth. Every muscle in his body ached. Once when they were in Turkey, one of the guys in his unit landed a severe case of food poisoning. He had ended up in the hospital with dehydration. Gunner slowly pushed himself up. His stomach rolled to let him know it was still there. Damn good thing, because he was pretty sure he'd managed to expel it and a few other internal organs last night—like his lungs, liver, intestines...fuck, he'd never been so sick in his entire life.

Weak and shaking, with a headache the size of the Pacific Ocean, he managed to lift himself into a sitting position on the floor. Light filtered in the bathroom's window curtain, so at least he'd made it through the night. It was touch and go there for a while. He remembered praying to the powers that be to just take him. Sooner or later he'd have to crawl out of this bathroom and face a woman he could have solid emotions for after almost dying in front of her toilet.

Hopefully, A.J. had left, or at least he prayed she had. He wanted no living witnesses to the things that happened in this little five-foot-by-ten-foot room last night. Hopefully, she would stay gone until he gathered enough strength to get up and...hell...yeah, so getting up was about as far as his mind or body were willing to stretch for an immediate goal. Even achieving that goal was dubious.

With single-minded determination, he pulled himself up onto the ledge of the tub. For at least thirty minutes, he and that ledge became fast friends. With a pat of thanks, he abandoned his ledge and pulled himself into a standing position against the vanity. Bracing himself against his next best friend, he concentrated on sucking air in and out of his lungs. Nausea lurked just out of the forefront, but if he moved faster than a slug, he'd be dry heaving again.

He heard a door in the house slam open and heavy footsteps head straight toward the bathroom door. A hard, loud knock rang like a bell inside his skull. "Holy fuck, what?" That was a whine. Damn it, he fucking whined. His hands grasped at his ears as if he could muffle the sound that had already penetrated it.

"Gunner, open the door, son." His father's voice held the "I'm not taking no for an answer" tone. He reached over and thumbed the lock. His father pushed the door open and gave him a once over. "Okay. I have my truck outside. We are going to the emergency room."

"No, I'm okay." Gunner swayed and took a swipe at the vanity a split second before he crashed into his old man.

"No, you're not. At a minimum you're dehydrated." His dad ducked under his arm and wrapped his arm around Gunner's waist. "You still nauseous? Can you make it to the truck?"

Gunner leaned against his dad. "I can make it." They stumbled through the door and out the front of the house. His dad wasn't lying. His truck was on the grass directly in front of the front door. Grinding his teeth together to prevent nausea from taking over, he let his dad help him into the truck and put his seatbelt on. Like a baby. He kept his eyes closed, the sun alone was enough to make him hurl.

The truck lunged forward, and Gunner slid down in the seat. "Why are you here? You're supposed to be in San Francisco."

"We spent the night. Drove home at a leisurely pace and had lunch before I took her home and came back. A.J. was waiting on my step for me. The girl looked like hell. She told me what happened."

"I think maybe she's trying to kill me." His attempt at humor probably fell flat, but fuck it, the woman must have had some kind of subconscious need to make sure she witnessed him at his worst.

Silas clucked his tongue like a mother hen. "She feels like shit."

Gunner laughed and immediately grabbed his gut and sides. He felt like his ribs had gone a couple hundred rounds with Muhammad Ali during the man's glory days. "I know that feeling."

"No, I don't think you do. She feels so bad she offered to sell back the shares of the Walrus to me." His father's anger at her offer was evident.

Gunner risked opening his eyes. He squinted at his father. "Why the fuck would she do that? I know she didn't mean to..." Gunner pushed his arms out to his side, grasping his father. "Pull over!" He scrambled for the door handle before he finished his words. The truck slammed to a stop a fraction of a second before he flung open the door and extended out of the cab. His father's hand caught the back of his slacks and held on while his body dry heaved.

Exhausted, he laid his head against the door handle. His dad pulled him back in and reached over him to slam the door shut. "I'm taking you into Redwood City. The Urgent Care is just going to send you there anyway."

"Don't let her sell, Dad." Gunner couldn't let her do that. He wanted her to stay.

"Didn't plan on it. I'll get her to come to the hospital so you can talk to her, okay?"

"Yeah, after...okay? After." He didn't want her to see him like this. He'd been through armed conflicts, been shot—twice, stabbed once, and had even broken his ankle on a training scenario, but he'd never felt as weak and useless as he did at this second. This was not how he wanted A.J. to see him. Ever.

"Why not now?" His dad's question made him cringe.

"I want to be able to tell her it wasn't her fault without fighting the need to throw up or sprint to the john. Just tell her to give me a couple hours." The docs had to have something that would settle his gut down. "I want to see her. Tell her that, just —not now."

Silas grunted his reluctant agreement. Silas thought he was making a mistake, but between a raging headache, constant nausea and gut-clenching episodes of...other bodily functions, he just couldn't care.

His father's hand on his arm startled him awake. "Come on, son." His dad helped him into the emergency room. Thirty minutes later, lying down in a semi-comfortable hospital bed with two syringes, one for nausea and one for his headache, pumped into the IV currently hooked into him, he took his first relaxed breath in over fifteen hours.

"You should have come in at the onset of symptoms." The doctor slid his finger along the edge of his tablet.

Gunner barely opened his eyes. He was exhausted, but he managed a snort. "There was no way I was leaving that bathroom doc."

The man lifted his eyes from the electronic chart

and blinked at him as if he'd just spoken Latin. Gunner let his lids fall. The world was feeling swirly. "What did you give me?"

"Something to relax you and let you sleep. Let the other medicine do its job. Your body isn't too happy with you just now." The doctor's voice floated to him.

"I need to talk to A.J." Mumbled, the sentence didn't sound as clear as it had in his head.

"Who is A.J.?" The doctor's voice was farther away.

Gunner tried to open his eyes but couldn't. He was so tired. "Mine. She's...mine."

CHAPTER 14

"*A*re you sure he asked for me?" A.J. trotted down the long hall of the hospital to keep up with Silas's loping strides.

"Positive." He turned the corner and stopped momentarily looking right and left. "Here, this way." He motioned to his right and took off down the hall again.

"Silas, is he okay?" She grabbed his arm and stopped the man.

Silas glanced down at her as if he didn't understand her question.

"Why are we practically running down the hall?" Her hand waved back and forth. "Is Gunner alright? God, did...did I...is he going to die?" Her heart stopped beating and her breath caught in her throat at the thought.

Silas looked at her like she had four heads. "No, definitely not. He'll be just fine. Doc said he was dehydrated. Gave him some meds for his headache and to stop nausea. Gave him something so he could rest. They figure he'll be walking out of here tomorrow morning." He glanced at his watch and then to her. "Truth is, I'm expected somewhere in about an hour, but I wanted to get you here and settled before I head back to Half Moon Bay. I'm sorry if I worried you."

A.J. let a little of the fifty-five-ton weight that had been grinding down on her slip away. He would be alright. She closed her eyes in silent prayer. *Thank you.* Opening her eyes, she squeezed Silas's arm. "I can find the room. If I get lost, I'll ask one of the nurses for directions. Go on. I'll be fine." Silas glanced from her to his watch. He glanced down at her again. "Go." She shooed him away.

Silas leaned down and kissed her on the cheek. "Room 6364. Call if you need anything?"

"I'll be fine. Go." She watched him walk to the corner and disappear. She checked the signs at the corner and glanced at the room numbers in front of her. She chuckled and headed back the other way. They'd been going in the wrong direction. She slowed as she passed the hallway Silas had walked down, looking to make sure the man turned at the right passage. She stood on her tiptoes and just managed to see him over a few people milling in the halls. She watched to make sure he headed out the correct way. She caught a movement in her peripheral vision. Two nurses were walking toward her. "Excuse me, room 6364?"

The older of the two nurses motioned down the hall. "See the nurse's station?"

A.J. nodded, "Yes, ma'am."

"I believe it is the one just past the station. Evens are on this side." She looked to the other nurse who nodded confirming her directions.

"Thank you." A.J. headed down the hall. She was anxious to see Gunner and terrified at the same time. *How could Gunner ever forgive her?*

She slowed as the numbers hit sixty and then sixty-two. A.J. slowly pushed the door open and peeked inside. Although it was a semi-private room, Gunner was alone. She slid through the door and made her way over to his bed. He was so pale. She stood beside his bed quietly, not wanting to disturb his sleep.

She wanted to touch his hand, to give him comfort, but what would he want? She worried her bottom lip and clutched the bed's aluminum rails. He'd asked her to leave last night. Silas laughed when she told him. *"Well, of course he did. What man wants the woman he fancies to hear him being sick?"*

"I didn't mean to do it, Silas. I worked all damn day on that meal. I tried so hard." She broke into tears and blubbered like a baby. Silas had held her and let her cry.

"Kiddo, that man cares for you as much as you care for him. Don't let this little hiccup set any distance between you." Silas rubbed her back as he spoke.

"I don't know. He was so sick and..."

"Hush. When I told him that you'd offered to sell back your shares of the Walrus, he was pissed. Told me to make sure I didn't let you sell. He cares. Trust me, he cares."

A.J. stood quietly beside his bed until her feet hurt. She memorized the angles of his face and admired the thick full lashes that rested on his cheeks. She knew women who would spend a fortune for lashes that long. His beard framed his lips. She moved to trace them but stopped short of touching him. He'd die of embarrassment if she ever told him, but he had a perfect cupid's bow upper lip and a full bottom lip. His smile. She glanced around the room pretty sure she wouldn't be the recipient of that smile for a long time. If ever again. Damn, she could sure mess things up.

The nurses who came in and checked Gunner's vitals were polite and professional. All reminded her she could pull the chair closer to the bed, but she declined. A.J. stood away from the bed when they came in and returned to her spot when they left.

When they weren't in the room, she'd couldn't resist thinking about the times she'd taken a good thing and turned it into dust. Marcus. That was the biggest question mark in her life. Maybe if she'd tried harder? She played the months of their relationship through her mind. No, she'd done everything she could. He tried to isolate her and make her feel bad about herself. She cared for the man and changed as much as she could, but there was a line she wouldn't cross. When she reached it, she broke up with him. There was nothing wrong with ending a relationship that wasn't working. Her father, her lawyer, and her sisters all told her that. Of course, that was after Marcus had tried to kill her.

A.J. took a deep breath and shook herself out of the past. The smells and sounds of the hospital were probably what caused her maudlin thoughts. The last time she'd been at a hospital she'd been a patient, not a visitor. The time displayed by the clock on the wall surprised her. It appeared she'd been lost in thought for longer than she'd realized. Interesting how a hospital room could induce reflection. Her eyes lingered on Gunner. He was an amazing man. Silas and his late wife had raised him well. She'd be lucky if he still talked to her when he woke up.

Glancing at the clock again, she conceded she probably needed to call an Uber and find a hotel room. Silas was covering the bar tonight. Staying close to the hospital made more sense than battling traffic in the morning. The sign on the wall said visiting hours were over in fifteen minutes. She'd wait until then and come back in the morning. Gunner wanted to see her, and although Silas assured her Gunner didn't want her to sell back her shares in the Walrus, that didn't mean the wide birth he'd given her before wouldn't come back into play. That would pierce her heart. She had fallen for the big Navy SEAL. Hook, line, sinker, fishing pole, boat, and ocean.

Gunner drew a deep breath and moved. He blinked and searched the ceiling as if trying to orient himself. His eyes flashed around the room, bouncing around until they landed on her. She gave him a tremulous smile and whispered, "Hi." She waited for him to say something. Anything.

He cleared his throat. "I'm sorry."

A.J. blinked rapidly trying to get her brain to understand those words. "What do you have to be sorry about? I'm the one who gave you food poisoning."

Gunner smiled and reached out, hesitating when the IV pulled on his hand. A.J. stepped forward and placed her hand in his. His fingers curled in and gently engulfed her hand. "I'm sorry that I ruined dessert." He smiled at her and made a valiant attempt at a wink.

Oh. Had he seen the lingerie hanging behind the bathroom door? She shook her head. It didn't matter. "Can you ever forgive me?" As she asked, she focused on their joined hands. He tugged on her hand to gain her attention.

"I forgave you the second I realized what happened. Your dinner was amazing. What you tried to do for me, was...hell, it was beyond anything anyone has ever...look I'm going to botch this up. Let me just tell you straight out, okay?"

A.J. braced herself mentally for whatever Gunner needed to say. She lowered her eyes to their joined hands and nodded.

"Hey, look at me." She lifted her eyes to his again. "There you go. I'm not sure what is going on between us, Amanda Jean Ericson, but I do know I have some deep feelings about you. Deeper than I've ever felt for anyone else. I don't know what to do with that revelation. I know I'm going to mess up occasionally. It is in my DNA. Just ask Pops." He smiled when she laughed. "But I figure I'm going to try, because what you did for me last night? You tried to give me a perfect dinner, and it was amazing."

A.J. rolled her eyes. "Until it wasn't."

"Until it wasn't." He agreed with her. "In the future when I try, and I fall short, and it isn't amazing, are you going to get mad and walk away from me?"

She shook her head vehemently. No, she wouldn't. That wasn't in *her* DNA.

"Then give me some credit, okay? I sent you away because I didn't need an audience. Was I trying to salvage just a little of my pride? Oh, hell yeah." A.J. chuffed out a bit of a laugh at that comment. "So, no more beating yourself up, yeah?"

"I'm so sorry." She stared at those deep brown eyes that were so dark against his pale skin. Even the tan he had couldn't disguise how ill her meal had made him. The dark brown of his beard made his pallor even more noticeable. "You were so sick."

"Because I ate enough to feed two SEAL teams. That'll teach me for being greedy." He pulled her hand up to his mouth and kissed the back of it. "I know telling you to stop worrying about it is probably useless, but let's get this behind us, okay?"

"I can do that if you let me take care of you when they release you from here. I've been told my chicken and dumplings are phenomenal and many people have consumed them with no ill effects." She glanced at him under her lashes hoping the humor wasn't ill-advised.

He laughed softly. "I'll eat anything you cook, except–"

"Mussels." They spoke the word at the same time.

"I swear I'll never cook mussels again." A.J. crossed her heart with her fingers.

"I swear I'll never eat your mussels again." He used his free hand to cross his chest.

Their laughter settled as they stared at each other. The kindness and soft emotion in his eyes held and trapped her gaze. He truly was an amazing man.

The moment was interrupted by an older gentleman in a white coat walking into the room. "Ah, I see you're awake. Feeling better?"

"Awesome. Not ready to run a marathon just yet, but I'm feeling better." A.J. tried to free her hand, but as his doctor loomed closer, Gunner held her hand, not allowing her to fade away.

"I've checked the vitals the nurses have annotated, they look good. Are you feeling any nausea?"

"No, no cramping either. Headache's gone. Just tired, now." Gunner started rubbing his thumb over the back of her hand. It sent a little shiver through her.

"Good, good." The doctor turned his attention to the tablet in his hand as he swiped and tapped. "Alright, we are going to keep you overnight. I want to make sure we don't have any other issues secondary to dehydration. The likelihood is minuscule, but I'm not prone to taking risks." A.J.'s eye's widened as she looked down at her hot SEAL. He was definitely a risk taker, after all, he was willing to stick it out with her. The doctor lowered the tablet. "I'll be around in the morning. If everything looks good, we'll release you and let you go home. Do you have someone at home?" The doctor gazed from Gunner to A.J.

"I'll be there," she answered for Gunner.

"Good. I'll leave instructions what he can have to limit nausea and get his system ready for his normal diet when I discharge him. I'm not overly concerned about any lingering effects, but we need to make sure someone is on hand."

"Thank you." A.J. stood silently as the doctor finished. Before the doctor left, he looked over his shoulder. "Visiting hours are over. The nurses don't get pushy about it for another half hour or so, but then they become rather intense." He glanced out the door. "I suggest you leave before they bring out the pitchforks."

A.J. laughed, and Gunner shook his head. A smile spread across his face before he spoke, "Noted.

Thanks, doc." Gunner waited until the door closed before he turned his worried gaze to her. "Are you driving back tonight?"

"No, I'm getting an Uber to the nearest hotel. I'll be back as soon as visiting hours start tomorrow. Silas will come get us as soon as I tell him you're being released." She ran her hand over his forehead. His eyes closed as she did. "You're tired. Go to sleep. I'll be here in the morning."

He nodded and didn't open his eyes again. Her hand remained in his, and she stroked through his hair until the nurses politely asked her to leave. There wasn't a pitchfork in sight.

CHAPTER 15

*G*unner rolled over and blinked at the white ceiling of his bedroom. He felt semi-human, which was a three thousand percent improvement from when he woke up two days ago on A.J.'s bathroom floor. He rubbed his hand over his chest, scratching it through the light smattering of hair. He glanced around his room. A.J. was here when he'd gone to sleep last night. He lifted on his elbows and looked for any signs she was still in the house. There was nothing of hers in his bedroom. No clothes or shoes. His stomach rumbled, but this time from hunger and not nausea.

He flipped the sheet and blanket off and headed into his en suite. He was disappointed she'd left without telling him. Yesterday, they'd had a quiet afternoon and evening after he'd been discharged. Silas had driven them home, made sure they had everything they needed and headed out. He was opening *and* closing the Walrus. Gunner hated his old man would have to pull a full shift, but Silas told him to shove a sock in it, reminding him he was more than capable of running his own pub for one night.

So, Gunner shoved a sock in it. He'd still worry, it just wouldn't be when his dad was around to hear it. Instead, he'd tucked A.J. into his side on the couch, and they'd had a Netflix marathon watching the British version of *Sherlock*. It was hard to understand the fast-paced English accent at first, but once they got into the series, the accent wasn't a factor. The show was head and shoulders better than the American version, at least in his opinion.

A.J. had made him broth and toast for dinner, and he ate it. Granted he was cautious, but not about her cooking. He was concerned about his body forcibly ejecting whatever he ate, no matter the source. The broth and toast stayed down, and he let her talk him into going to sleep about ten last night. They'd done nothing more than snuggle together under the covers. His mind wanted more, but he settled for holding her close. *She'd slept with me, right?* He could remember pulling her closer during the middle of the night. *But where was she now?*

Done in the bathroom, he shuffled to the bedroom door and opened it. The marvelous aroma of coffee smacked him upside the head. He followed that scent like a hound chasing a fox. As he rounded the corner, he paused. A.J. stood at his kitchen window, coffee cup in hand, staring out toward the bay. He glanced past her and smiled. His dad and Charlotte were on the beach looking out at the water. He assumed if Charlotte was here this early, she'd probably come home with his dad and spent the night. His father had her tucked protectively against his side. Gunner padded up next to A.J. and put his arm over her shoulder, duplicating his father's stance.

A.J. leaned her head against his chest. "Did I wake you?"

"I think you being gone woke me, but I've slept enough in the last two days. The coffee smells fantastic."

"I'll get you some." A.J. stopped after she retrieved a cup and glanced at him. "Is your stomach ready to handle coffee?"

"Most definitely. That and a couple slabs of bacon and maybe a stack of pancakes three-feet tall smothered in maple syrup." Gunner took the cup from her hand and poured it himself.

She motioned toward the beach. "I can make breakfast for all of us. Do you think we should invite them?"

Gunner glanced out the window at the exact time his dad kissed Charlotte. He closed his eyes and shook his head. He never wanted to think about his father doing that ever again. "No, I think they are just fine by themselves." He opened his eyes and winked at her before took a sip of his coffee. "But, I'll let you cook for me."

"You'll *let* me, huh?" She laughed at his joke before

she became quiet and pensive. He took another sip of his coffee and waited. "Are you sure?" Her words were soft, but sorrow dripped off them. She pulled her bottom lip into her mouth and chewed on it.

He sat his cup down and turned her so she faced him. He tucked his thumb and forefinger under her chin before he used his thumb to pull her lower lip from her teeth. "I'm positive. We aren't going to go there anymore. Remember? Water under the bridge." He spun her around and pointed her toward the refrigerator. "I'll cook tomorrow. It's fair to take turns." Although he couldn't cook for shit, he'd try like crazy if it made her happy.

She grimaced when she glanced over her shoulder at him but kept walking across the kitchen. "How about *I* cook, and *you* clean?" She opened the cupboard and put her hands on her hips. "Dammit," A.J. muttered quietly, spun and looked around the kitchen.

"I have a master's degree in cleaning, or at least I should as much as the Navy liked making us perfect that skill." He watched her as she went into the laundry room. He lifted his voice so she would hear him, "What are you doing?"

She hollered back at him, "I'm looking for a step stool."

Gunner padded toward the laundry room. The door abruptly shut in front of him, missing his nose by a fraction of an inch. It whipped back open again.

She stormed out and headed toward the garage. "A.J.?"

She spun around, walking backward as she spoke, "Yes?"

"I don't have a step stool."

She stopped walking. Her brow furrowed as she shot a pissed off look towards the cupboard. "Okay. I'll buy one the next time I go shopping."

"Why?" Gunner followed her gaze toward the kitchen cabinets. He literally had no idea what was upsetting her, or maybe frustrating her.

She pointed toward the cupboard as if it had offended her, and then stared at him like the answer to his question was obvious.

He rubbed his face trying to wake up because his mind was not keeping up with her this morning. "I give. I've always sucked at charades. How about you just tell me what you're pointing at?"

She placed her hands on her hips and cocked her head toward the cabinet as she spoke. "I can't reach the flour or the baking powder, or any of the ingredients I need to make you pancakes."

Gunner glanced at the shelves. "Okay. I'll get you what you need and keep you company while you cook. When we have time, we can rearrange them, so you don't need a step stool."

"You'd do that?" She moved over to the counter and waited for him.

"Get you the flour and baking powder? Sure." He

reached over her, easily grabbed the containers she named, and put them down on the counter.

"No, I meant rearranging your cabinets." She opened the fridge and grabbed the milk, eggs, and butter.

"Yeah, why wouldn't I?" Gunner reached for his coffee and took a sip.

"You're willing to rearrange your house to accommodate me?" She opened another door and looked at the shelves. She pointed to the top. "Glass measuring cup, please."

Gunner reached over her, grabbed the cup and placed it on the counter. He stopped her from turning away from him and pulled her between his legs. "What you fail to realize is that I want you in my life, A.J. I'd try to stop the rotation of the earth for you. I'm fully vested in this relationship. Are we off to a rocky start? Yeah. But that has gone to prove how much I do care about you. I didn't bail then, I'm not going pop the cord now, either. You are worth the effort. Hopefully, you feel the same way."

She blinked at him. "Pop the cord?"

He made a motion across his chest. "Bailing out of an aircraft, opening your chute. Popping the cord."

Her eyes widened in understanding. "Oh."

Oh. Just, oh? He cleared his throat. "You do feel the same way, right?"

"I do." She smiled up at him. "But it is really good to hear you say it."

Thank God. "Are you hungry?" Gunner kissed her neck as he asked.

She shivered under his caress and murmured a breathless, "No. Wait, I mean yes."

He chuckled as he drew his lips along the column of her neck. "Which is it?" He breathed the words behind her ear in the exact spot he'd found to be one of her erogenous zones when they'd made love before.

"Yes. Hungry for you." Her hands snaked around his neck. "Starving."

"Well, then let's take care of that." He straightened, and her arms drifted down his chest. He captured one hand and lifted it to his lips, kissing it as he backed her down the hallway to his room. It was quite possibly the longest twenty seconds of his life.

He lifted the cotton edge of her t-shirt and pulled it off. She smiled at him and reached behind to unfasten and slip off her bra. Rose colored nipples hardened under his touch. He dropped to his knees in front of her. A.J.'s hands ran through his hair as he looked up at her. "You are beautiful, inside and out." The truth of the words flooded through him. He leaned forward, kissing her stomach.

"So are you." Her hands cupped his face as he drew back.

He chuckled, "Don't ever let my team hear you say that." All thoughts of conversation dissipated into thin air. He let his tongue and mouth play as he unfastened her jeans and slid them down her legs.

The barely-there piece of satin he found under the denim lasted two seconds before he had her naked. He stood and possessed her mouth while he maneuvered her into his bed and underneath him. Her warm kisses welcomed him back into her embrace, and he reveled in the wonder of that gift. Gunner lifted up long enough to gaze at her. He wanted the image of her flushed face, swollen lips and heavily hooded eyes permanently etched in his brain.

She ran her hands up and down his arm. "Make love to me."

Gunner lowered to kiss her tenderly, speaking in between soft swipes of his lips against hers. "I will if you make love to me." He wanted to be sure they were on the same page. Communication between them needed to be crystal clear.

"For as long as you'll let me." She wrapped her arms around his neck.

"Then forever it is." Gunner silenced whatever she was going to say with a kiss that he prayed showed her how much she meant to him. He pressed his body against hers, touching as much skin as he could.

His need to possess her body and claim her as his own burned brighter than any desire he'd ever experienced. The feel of A.J.'s skin under his hands, the warmth of her sensual lips on his were gasoline on the fire her mere presence ignited and stoked his desire into a raging flame of intensity.

She rubbed her entire naked length against his body. He fucking shuddered, the sensation of her hard nipples against his chest adding more fuel to his already insane need. She lifted her arm and wrapped her hand around the back of his neck. He lowered to kiss the sweet spot just below her ear. She leaned her head away giving him complete access. "You remember when I told you there would be a time for urgency?" "Ummm...I do remember that. Could this be the time?" She leaned her head back and tipped her eyes up to make contact with his.

"It is definitely the time." He stopped and glanced toward the drawer of his nightstand. "I'm going to have to leave you for a moment." Her hand on his arm stilled him. "I don't need them if you tell me we're okay without them. I'm on birth control."

"I swear I'm good to go. I was tested regularly for everything while I was in the Navy." He dropped his lips to her neck again. That little gasp she made lit him up. Fuck, she was so responsive to his touch.

"I was checked several times in the hospital before I left Texas. You were the first...since."

He moved slightly so he could bring his mouth over hers in a sloppy, needy, hot-as-fucking-hell, kiss. As soon as his lips left hers, he growled, "I'm the only one from now on."

"God, yes," she agreed as he flipped her to her stomach and pulled on her hips.

"Hands and knees, babe."

She braced herself on her arms and glanced back at him. "Bring it on sailor boy. Rock my world."

He brought them together. Her mind-numbingly

tight heat gloved his cock. She pushed back against him, demanding without words. She was perfection, rocking as he thrust. They exploded when they met. The compulsion of his body overrode his desire to draw the union out. Their bodies fucking melded together. A.J. gasped, then tightened around his cock. Her guttural moan filled the room. He grabbed her hips and rode through his climax.

He withdrew and she collapsed on the bed with a moan. He lay next to her and carefully rolled her to her back. He moved the thick fall of auburn hair away from her face so he could see her. "You okay?"

She opened her eyes and crossed them comically with a vigorous nod, then closed them again and snuggled into his arms. He lingered over her, kissing her with lazy, languid strokes of his tongue. The intimacy of this moment was on a level he'd never experienced. He wasn't virtuous. He'd slept around, but he'd never had this—the connection, the emotion, the need to protect and to cherish.

Lying together, they let their hands roam, touch, caress and learn. Nothing overtly sexual, just two people enjoying each other.

"Tell me about them?" A.J. tilted her head so he could see her face as she spoke.

"Who?" "Your team. You've mentioned them before." She reached back, grabbed the blanket, and covered both of them.

"They are some of the best men on the planet." He lifted the arm she wasn't laying on, above his head and propped himself up a bit. He stared up at the ceiling and thought about the men that served with him. Each of them had sacrificed for their country, individually and through the years, together. They'd all sweated blood as they accomplished missions no one would ever know about. He smiled to himself because that was as it should be. A.J.'s fingertips against his chest drew his mind back to her question. "They are my brothers, if not by genetics then by choice. Not a single one of them has good taste, though."

She lifted up on her elbow, a cascade of auburn hair falling around her shoulders. "What?"

"Well considering we run a pub, what would you say about a guy who walked in and ordered a Salty Dog?" Chase loved those fucking grapefruit drinks.

A.J. laughed. "Some people like the bitterness."

"Yeah, I guess it takes all types. Chase can down those sour things." Gunner wrinkled his nose. "We have the waitresses and bar staff hopping when we're together."

"Well, I know you prefer single malt." She straddled him, lying on her stomach on his chest with her hands cupped under her chin. "There had to be a bourbon or whiskey drinker, right?"

"Yeah, Asher drinks bourbon, neat. No ice."

A.J. chuckled, "Smart man. Who wants to pay for ice?"

151

"Right?" Gunner laughed with her. "Hell, the places we were deployed to, the water was sketchy. Ice wasn't always a good bet."

She snorted and glanced up at him. "No doubt. What other types of drinks? Am I going to have to learn to make something exotic if these guys come to visit?"

Gunner shook his head. "Maybe, Clay drinks dirty martinis. Carson loves Sex on the Beach."

A.J. lifted her chin off her hands in surprise. "You mean vodka and peach schnapps, that kind of sex on the beach?"

Gunner grimaced. "Shit I hope so, actual sex on a beach is one gritty fuck." He got a smack on the shoulder for that comment, but A.J. laughed with him anyway.

"Let's see, Nikko is easy. He drinks beer. Trevor only drinks coffee."

"Yeah? Why?" She lay on his chest, her cheek pressed against his pec.

"Why only coffee?"

She nodded her head as he played with her hair.

"I don't know. He's not a drinker. I assumed he had his reasons. We all respected it." He lifted her hair and let it drop slowly. "Then there is Red. Noah Seager. The man drinks red wine."

A.J. lifted her head enough to raise an eyebrow at him. "Really?"

"Uh huh. No shit. Crazy, I know." She let out a small laugh as she lay back down. He could feel her body relaxing on top of him. "Conner is the last of the group. He drinks Rusty Nails."

A.J lifted her finger but didn't move. Her voice emerged sleepy. "I like Rusty Nails. Drambuie and scotch. What's not to like?" Her hand drifted down to his shoulder as her breathing deepened and evened out.

Gunner smiled to himself. What's not to like? Nothing. Life was fucking perfect.

CHAPTER 16

A.J. looked up from the book she was reading on her phone and once again glanced out the front window at the deserted Main Street. The rain was coming down hard. It was an evil night even though she and Gunner were working together. He'd taken over Tessa's shift after the woman eloped with a certain police officer. The happy couple would be back next week. In the meantime, she and Gunner worked together, and Silas worked with August. It was a perfect schedule and had given them all plenty of time off.

The rain swept the pavement in sheets as she watched. Nobody had ventured out in the storm, and they should be closing up, even though it was early. She'd already wiped everything down, and kept herself occupied at the front of the house, while Gunner cussed and fumed in the back. Tonight, he was finishing his build of a new shelving system in the storage room. She'd learned pretty fast asking if she could help would only end up with her watching from two feet away rather than twenty as he worked and cussed and fumed.

It had been three months since he'd returned to Half Moon Bay. A month and a half since she'd almost killed him. Near death via mussels. It was a thing. She chuckled and shook her head. She would never forgive herself for that, but what they had together since then was amazing.

Gunner's phone rang. She could hear the ringtone, a croaking bullfrog, clearly. She had no idea why he liked the sound, but she guessed it held some significance to him.

The cussing stopped. "Say what?" Another pause. "No, I didn't. Seriously, I couldn't have heard you right. Repeat it?"

She slid off the stool where she'd been sitting and headed back to the storeroom. Gunner was sitting on his heels, hammer and shelf beside him. She took in the space around her. *Oh, dang, the shelving unit was impressive.*

"You're fucking with me, right?" Gunner looked up at her and smiled. A wide, happy smile. "When?" He looked down at the floor and then at his watch. He cupped the phone against his ear and swiped his watch bringing up the calendar. "Soooo...a week, huh?" Gunner laughed. "A week! Dude, how the fuck does that happen in seven days?" He listened some more. "Well, listen Red, you and...I'm sorry, what's her name again?" Gunner paused. "Right. You and Ellie come on out, any time. We need to catch up, and I have someone I want you to meet." He laughed and winked at A.J. "Not telling you shit until you get your ass out here. I have a small rental house on our property, right on Half Moon Bay. Consider it a honeymoon or something like that." Gunner listened for a while longer. "Am I the first one you've called?" He threw back his head and laughed hard. "Right. Consider the invite open-ended. I don't envy you those calls, man." He listened for a minute longer and laughed again. "Congratulations, I'm happy for you. Get your ass out here." Gunner pulled the phone away from his ear, put it one of the completed shelves, and turned towards her.

"Good news?" A.J. leaned against the door jamb and kept an eye on the front of the house in case some adventurous soul braved the storm for a drink.

A smirk spread across his face. "My friend, Noah, got married."

"Noah, the red wine drinker?" It had become a game matching up the drinks to the names of his teammates when he talked about them.

"Yeah, the kicker is, he got married a week after he got out. But, wait for it...he wasn't seeing anyone when he got out." Gunner shook his head and chuckled.

A.J. had to digest that one for a second. "A week, huh? Wow, I thought *we* were moving quickly. Married in a week? That's impressive."

"Right? I guess she was his high school sweetheart, or he knew her in high school? I didn't really catch all of it. He was talking fast."

"I heard you invite them out here." She lifted her eyebrows and waited for his response.

"Yeah, I'd like you to meet him. Well, them." Gunner slid the last shelf into place. The practicality of the design was impressive.

A.J. waited until he looked back at her and gave him a pointed look. "Uh huh. You offered them my house."

Gunner stood, put the hammer on the shelf with his phone and then drew her into his arms. "You do kinda live with me, already. It would take a single afternoon this weekend to move the rest of your stuff over."

"Aww...you are such a romantic! Is that your way of asking me to move in with you? Inviting your friends to honeymoon in my house?" A.J. blinked up at him.

"Maybe. Should I have fancied it up?" He squinted at her like she was a jigsaw puzzle and he was looking for the right piece.

She squinted back at him. "Maybe. But I'll let you off the hook."

He perked up at that. "Yeah?" His face split with a beautiful smile.

She shook her head looking up at him. He was such a man-child at times. "Yeah, but only because I love you."

Gunner had been leaning in for a kiss when she said the words. He froze. His eyes darted to hers. "Say that again."

A.J. steeled herself and repeated her words, "I love you."

She shrieked when Gunner let out a 'whoop' and swept her into his arms spinning her around. He dropped her to her feet and cupped her face in his hands. "You don't know how many times I wanted to say that to you." His mouth dropped to hers and he kissed her until she was dizzy and clinging to him for balance.

Gunner drew up and looked around, still holding her in his arms. "We need to close up. There's nobody here, and nobody is coming out in this weather."

A.J. stepped back when he loosened his embrace. The fact he hadn't said it back to her niggled at her, but his reaction said volumes, so she'd let it go. For now.

He spun her and pointed her toward the bar with a slap on the butt. "I'm going to sweep up in here. Could you bring back the trash? I'll take it out with the scraps and other stuff. No need getting drenched more than once."

"Ah...sure." A.J. headed to the front of the bar, slightly off balance and one hundred percent elated. Gunner's happy whistle followed her down the hall. Would she ever totally understand that man?

A.J. emptied the small amount of trash behind the bar and took it to the back. The rain had abated a bit.

She agreed with Gunner. No one would venture out at nine-thirty on a rain-soaked night to have a drink, so she punched her code into the register and started the process of ringing the cash register out for the night.

The bell over the front door tinkled. A.J. glanced up from the register and froze. Marcus's brother Mitchell stood inside the door. A sinister sneer spread across his face. "Did you think we wouldn't find you?" His held his right hand behind his back as stalked closer with a menacingly slow pace that terrified her. She glanced down the hall but snapped her eyes back toward Mitchell.

"You sisters are shit about keeping your whereabouts quiet. Rumor has it you bought into this place." He withdrew a baseball bat. "What right do you have moving on when Marcus is stuck in the Penn? He's fucking stuck on laundry room detail. Do you know what that means? Do you know what happens to men who work in the laundry room? They end up as prison whores."

A.J. shook her head. Her heart slammed against her chest as her mind raced. *How could she get him to leave? How could she warn Gunner?*

She glanced down the hallway. "Worried about that bartender? Don't. Malcolm is making sure we have more than enough time alone."

The back door slammed open and Gunner strode through with a ferocious snarl. She knew Gunner could see her, pushed back against the wall. She shook her head. *No, please, God, she didn't want him to get hurt. Not because of her.*

Gunner stalked down the hallway. He didn't hesitate for a second. He didn't ask any questions. He advanced on Mitchell. Mitchell pulled the bat back to swing. A.J. shouted, and Gunner stepped in close and threw a quick jab, snapping Mitchell's head back. Blood squirted across his face. Gunner's muscles flexed, and he twisted. There were solid thuds and sounds A.J. never wanted to hear again. It literally took seconds for Gunner to send the man sprawling toward the floor. He landed in a heap at Gunner's feet, and Gunner wasn't even breathing heavy, but he was pissed. Fury radiated off of him. He glanced over at her and she saw the transformation from enraged warrior to Iceman. His voice was calm, and he became tranquil. Like a switch flipped inside him. "A.J., honey, call the police."

She jumped and grabbed her phone. Her hands shook violently as she pushed the three numbers on her cell. She watched as Gunner picked up the bat and nudged Mitchell with the toe of his boot. The man didn't move.

Gunner shook his head as he spoke, "Glass jaw. Figures."

A woman answered, "Nine-one-one do you have—"

"Yes, I have a fucking emergency!" A.J. cut her off. "A man was here to attack me."

The calm, placid tone asked, "Where's here ma'am?"

A.J. snapped, "The Wayward Walrus. Main Street."

The woman had a little more urgency in her voice when she asked, "Is he still there, are you safe?"

"Yeah, Gunner knocked him out. There's another one in the back alley." She glanced at Gunner who had rolled Mitchell onto his side. Blood leaked from the man's nose.

"Tell her to send an ambulance. He's unconscious, the other one has a broken knee."

"He said to..."

"Yes ma'am, I heard. The police should..."

"They're here." Three cars slid almost simultaneously to the curb in front of the bar. The officers ran in, guns drawn. Gunner held up his hands, and so did she, her phone still in her hand.

A.J. spoke as soon as the officers stopped shouting. "I have a restraining order against him." A.J. chanced to lower her hand a bit to point at Mitchell. "He had a baseball bat and was threatening me. Gunner rescued me."

The last of the officers left and A.J. locked the door behind them. He watched her lean against the door for a moment before she braced her shoulders and turned back to him. She walked across the front of the bar to where he sat on a stool with his hand stuck in a bowl of ice—one she demanded he put his fist into. He complied, because just maybe she needed to be in charge of something tonight. Most everything was spinning by her at warp speed. His little firecracker was hovering over him, and he was okay with that. When she stood across from him, he pulled his fist out of the bucket of ice. A.J. took it in her hands and examined the bruising. It was minimal. He'd done worse just fucking around.

"He said my sisters were talking about where I lived. I never thought to ask them not to say anything." She dabbed antiseptic on the broken skin.

"From what Delmont told me, this will be the third strike for both of those assholes. Both have committed violent felonies in the past. Because they'll be tried in California, not Texas, they are looking at twenty-five-years to life. You'll never have to worry about them again." Or at least he hoped. He'd pull some strings and find a way to make sure he was notified if any of those men received early release. If they were stupid enough to come back to Half Moon Bay, Gunner would be waiting for them.

"Why did you turn him onto his side?" A.J. reached back for a clean bar towel.

"Because he could have aspirated his own blood. Lungs don't tolerate that well." Gunner wasn't going to jail, not for that scum. Self-defense was one thing, but with his extensive training, a good attorney might try to pin a negligent homicide tag on him. He didn't think the ex's family could afford a good attorney, but he wasn't going to risk it.

"You were pretty badass, you know." She peeked up at him through her lashes.

"I was, huh?" He leaned forward and waggled his eyebrows. Those morons weren't a serious threat to anyone but themselves, but he'd take the honors she bestowed upon him. He didn't even work up a sweat dispatching either of the fuckers. The only challenge had been to stop hitting the man threatening A.J. The urge to make them go away permanently was real. Thank God for his training. The self-discipline the Navy had ingrained in him was the only thing that allowed him to stop.

"Yeah. You are my knight in shining armor." She leaned forward and kissed him. "What do I give such a valiant savior as a reward?"

Gunner smiled across the bar at the woman he loved. "That's easy, my lady. I'll settle for nothing less than your heart. I love you."

The End.